Relentless

A Family's Struggle to Survive

HELEN FLEMING JOHNSON

Copyright © 2024 Helen Fleming Johnson.

All rights reserved. No part of this book may be reproduced, stored, or transmitted by any means—whether auditory, graphic, mechanical, or electronic—without written permission of both publisher and author, except in the case of brief excerpts used in critical articles and reviews. Unauthorized reproduction of any part of this work is illegal and is punishable by law.

ISBN: 979-8-89419-091-4 (sc)
ISBN: 979-8-89419-092-1 (hc)
ISBN: 979-8-89419-093-8 (e)

Because of the dynamic nature of the Internet, any web addresses or links contained in this book may have changed since publication and may no longer be valid. The views expressed in this work are solely those of the author and do not necessarily reflect the views of the publisher, and the publisher hereby disclaims any responsibility for them.

One Galleria Blvd., Suite 1900, Metairie, LA 70001
(504) 702-6708

DEDICATION

For my forefathers, grandparents, Rev. Mark E. and Mrs. Charity Smith, parents Mr. Walker and Mrs. Ruby Flemi7ng, my sister Ms. Ruby Bridgeforth and my beloved aunt Mrs. Artelure Gamble who thought we could fly!

Illustration: Nozomi Ann Johnson

CONTENTS

Chapter 1   Mariah 1
Chapter 2   News, News, News 7
Chapter 3   The Town 14
Chapter 4   Winds of Hope 20
Chapter 5   Decisions 29
Chapter 6   Strange Things 38
Chapter 7   Family Ties 44
Chapter 8   Trapped! 49
Chapter 9   The Morning Crier 55
Chapter 10   Riding with the Devil 66
Chapter 11   Camden 71
Chapter 12   Beck Spur 75
Chapter 13   Stolen 78
Chapter 14   Hurting Deep Within My Soul 85
Chapter 15   Bitter Fruit 98
Chapter 16   Just Before Dawn 106
Chapter 17   New Beginnings 136
Chapter 18   High Hopes 140

CHAPTER ONE

Mariah

Daniel went about his chores as he did on most mornings. He was fifteen and his brother William was eleven. They lived on a two-hundred-member slave plantation in North Carolina. The boys were not allowed to live in the weaver's slave cabin with their mother, nor were they allowed to call Mariah, mama. For as long as they could remember they had lived in a small room in the barn. Often, they were cold and wet and would sleep with the horses to keep warm. They shared this barn room with old Pete, who took care of them and the horses. The boys called him Grand Papa Pete, but so did everyone else. Thus, they did not know if he was their grandfather or not but they did know they were brothers and it was better to sleep in the barn than in the slave cabins.

Both boys were expert riders and knew how to care for and train horses. Some said they were like Old Grand Papa Pete, who had a sixth sense around horses, and they were becoming some of the best horse trainers in the county. Often Daniel and William rode the plantation's best horses during horse races for their owner. They would travel over the countryside from race to race with the plantation owner, Master Ed Smith. More often than not, they won. When they won a race there would be a little money, food, and a good time for all. But sometimes when they lost a race, Ed Smith would go into a rage and they would be severely beaten and not given food for several days.

Grand Papa Pete, warned the boys, "You are just slaves and can be kilt or sold at the whim of the master. Be careful around Master Ed Smith—he can be as cruel as they come. Be wise when you go to the races. Do not drink spirits or gossip with the other jockeys. Remember, you are only as valuable as your last win. If a master cannot pay his gambling debt, he will sell a slave and that might be you! You cannot think Master Smith is your friend just because some say he is your daddy. Daddy or not he will sell you if need be. And William, the older you get the more you look like Master Smith. That is a very dangerous thang! Slave masters do not want slave children' running around their plantation looking like them. William, you could almost pass for white. That alone puts you in danger!

"Stay away from the Big House! If the master's wife gets a good look at you, she will sell you for sure. Keep your hair cut short and that cap pulled down over your face. She does not know anything about her husband and Mariah.

"Master Smith married that ugly woman for her money and the hope of having *legitimate white children*. On most days he treats her really bad, but when he is drunk it is worse—he slaps her around. Calls her a whore! And tells her she was not pure when they were wed! Swears he has taken enough slave virgins to bed to know she was not a virgin when they were married! Worst of all he calls her the 'barren bitch,' and complains that they have been married six years and no children. She has become bitter and mean! And she will take out her anger on any slave . Beware! She sold Erma Jean's child because she thought that the poor little girl was Master Smith's daughter. The little girl will always wear the whipping scars she gave her on her face. Stay away from Mrs. Eva! Do you understand!"

"We will," said the boys.

The summer of 1860 turned into fall. The boys raced horses at various events. And they would go with Grand Papa Pete from plantation to plantation treating animals who had various diseases and repairing saddles, blinders, bits, and harness. Master Ed, on the advice of Dr. Baker, even allowed Old Pete to add a small room with a fireplace to the back of the barn with a door that had access to the north field so that old Pete and the boys could gather and dry the plants and herbs needed to treat the horses without going through the barn or slave quarters. The boys gathered comfrey, garlic, nettle, and other plants for the horses and hung these from the roof of the barn room to dry by the fireplace.

One of their favorite jobs was to help Pete make corn liquor and elderberry wine. After the wine and liquor were made, they would go from place to place "delivering the product." The product was what refined white women called corn liquor. They did not want anyone to know they drank corn liquor, and would go to great measures to hide the fact they were buying and drinking "moonshine." Their acts of deception were funny to William and Daniel, especially the many ways the pastor's wife could find to hide "shine." Once she hid a bottle of moonshine under her Sunday hat and went into the church for Sunday service. Old Grand Papa Pete always would bring the money earned from the sales back to Master Smith.

Periodically, they would slip out of the barn at night to visit their mother at the weaver's cabin. She was a tall, beautiful, mulatto woman with long, thick brown hair. She made fine lace, and weaved and dyed fabric and baskets. The boys would bring her moss and walnut leaves to make her dyes. Sometimes she would have a bit of food to share with them. She would say, "Boys, remember, we are enslaved people but we are not slaves. Never let anyone enslave your mind. Think! Think! It is the only way to survive this harsh thang called slavery. Keep learning your craft. And each time you leave the plantation, learn what is in each direction. Make a mental map of the county. Remember north is the road to freedom. One day you may be able to use this information. Do not wear your emotions for others to see. I pray one day we will all be free!"

One night when they were visiting, she said, "It is not safe for you to come here anymore. I will meet you at the Hush Harbor when I can." The Hush Harbor was a church they had built from sticks and twigs in the forest. "I will send you word by Grand Papa Pete when it is safe for us to meet, or if you see my broom hanging above the door, then I will meet you at the Hush Harbor. You are getting too big to come here. If anyone asks you if I am your mother, say, 'No, our mother was sold long ago, so they say. We do not remember our mother.' William, *do not* come to the Big House anymore, especially if there are guests. You look too much like Master Ed. You hear! You must obey me! Let Daniel come."

"Mama!" William cried.

"Do not call me mama, William—call me Mariah! Or Aunty Mariah.

"Daniel and I look the same except for our skin color."

"Yes, child, I know, but the whites see mostly skin color. Do as your mama said and do not come to the Big House. Stay out of sight of Master's wife. Remember, do not call me mama, just call me Mariah or Aunty Mariah. If you do have to come to the Big House, put grease from the wagon wheels mixed with dirt on your face, neck, and hands. Winter will be here soon. Hopefully, things will settle down. But there is talk of a war coming to the south in the spring."

The boys did not see their mother in August, September, nor in October. They missed her, but they were busy with the livestock, cleaning the barn and barnyard, training and caring for horses, horseraces, making corn liquor, and collecting herbs and medicinal plants. Most nights they were so tired when they came back to the barn, they just fell asleep.

Early one morning in November Daniel saw his mother running toward the barn. Her brown hair was flowing in the wind like a horse's mane. When he saw her hair was not covered, he was afraid that she would be punished. Slave women who failed to keep their hair covered could be beaten. It was a law. She ran toward Daniel and fell to the floor when she entered the barn.

"Where is Pete?" she cried.

"He and William went to the north pasture to check on the horses. Mama, what is wrong?"

"Slave auction! Slave auction! Master Smith arranged it in New Orleans a few weeks ago. I just overheard about it yesterday, when I was working at the Anderson Plantation. There will be a slave auction here any week now. But Mrs. Eva don't know nothing about it. Stay close to your brother. If you are sold, I hope you will be sold together. *Baby, I love you*!" She handed him two small bags tied to long strings. "Here, put this bag around your neck and this other bag around your brother's neck."

"Why? What is it?"

"It is an asafetida bag. This bag contains medicine. Use it if you get sick. Make a strong tea and drink it. Also sewn in the lining of the bag at the very bottom are three ten-dollar gold pieces. Master Smith gave them to me when you were born. I have been saving them to buy my freedom. But now . . ."

"Now what, Mama?"

"I am giving the coins to you for safekeeping. Let your mama hug you one last time. Hug your brother for me too. Don't tell anyone about the gold coins, not even William. Wait until he is much older."

"Mama, is Master Smith my daddy and William's daddy?" She hung her head and said nothing. "I bet if he was our daddy, he would free us."

"No! No!" she said. "He will not. I have asked him many times to set us free and he will not! Will not—you hear! It is sad but true. Slave masters have a lot of half-breed children. They do not free them. It is a lie for you to think so. And if Master's wife, Mrs. Eva, found out or even thought that he was your father, she would see you dead before night or sold. I saw what she did to poor Mary's baby. She sent Mary to gather vegetables from the garden, then drowned that little baby in the washtub. The baby had just begun to sit up, and he had red hair like Master Ed. I heard her tell her sister that she thought Mary's child was fathered by Master and she would not allow any half breed "nigger" children claiming her husband as Pa. *Never, never, tell anyone that you think Master is yours and William's daddy.* You hear! It could mean your death and mine too. Do not say anything about the slave auction! Wait for Pete! And tell him what I said. Remember, do not tell anyone else, not even your brother."

She hugged him again, looked out the barn door to see if anyone was there, covered her hair, and ran down the path to the weaver's cabin.

CHAPTER TWO

News, News, News

Grand Papa Pete and William had not returned to the barn. It had been three days. They had gone to town to send a telegram for Mrs. Eva Smith and she had said to wait until they received an answer from her father. "What a week!" Daniel thought. Nothing was normal about it.

Monday had started as a wonderful fall morning. It was unseasonably warm, dry, and peaceful. It was a great late November morning! The trees were still filled with color. Daniel thought he had never seen such beautiful red, orange, and brown leaves. Miss Amy, the master's sister-in-law, called it Indian Summer. North Carolina sure could be beautiful!

As he walked and did his morning chores, a small gust of wind blew the branches of the trees and leaves of various colors fell all around him. The bright colors looked wonderful on his mahogany skin. Oh! What a beautiful world God had created. For a moment he blocked out all of the misery of slavery and the gnawing hungry pain he felt in his stomach.

When he passed through the slave quarters the girls all smiled and some of the older girls teased him. Brass Mary Ann said, "Daniel, Daniel you sho' is handsome, standing six feet or more, broad shouldered, small waisted, and those powerful arms—and not to mention all those fine silky black curls. It is a shame you are only fifteen!" She shook her hips and said, "Too young for a woman like me. Hum, I guess these poor girls will have to wait a few more years before you grow up and become a man." She laughed and he smiled and kept walking. Mary Ann was nothing but trouble! And he knew it.

As he approached the kitchen of the Big House with eggs he had gathered, he heard screams and cursing like he had never heard before. There was so much loud cursing coming from the good little white Christian ladies on this fine warm November day. What in the world could be the problem? Mrs. Eva was cursing at the top of her lungs. She sounded like a drunken sailor, worse than the women at the whore houses in town when they did not get paid by a caller. If she had been a child, one would say she was having a temper tantrum and needed her mouth washed with lye soap!

Daniel eased through the kitchen door and placed the basket of eggs on the table. He was about to leave when Aunty Jenny, the cook, ran into the kitchen followed by a housemaid.

"Lord Jesus save us," she said as she rung her hands in her apron.

"What is going on Aunty Jenny?" asked Daniel.

"Well, baby it all started this morning. At about five thirty a.m., a rider came to the Big House with a message for Master Smith's wife, Mrs. Eva." The slaves called her Evil Eva. She was an ugly woman in spirit and body. She was tall and weighed about 250 pounds. Most days she made those around her miserable. Daniel often wondered why Master had married her and not her sister, who was pretty and reasonably kind.

"When she heard the message, she began weeping and wailing," Aunty Jenny continued. "Snot was flying out her nose everywhere. And tell you the truth, she was foaming at the mouth. I thought she was having a fit—one of them seizures!

"She was saying thangs like, 'He lost all my money! Lost my property! My jewels! Low life! White trash!' and so on. She was beside herself. Ain't never saw such yelling and cursing from a genteel white woman—and I have had more than three owners. She broke dishes and threw the master's clothes in the fire. Took a whip to young George for no reason. It seemed as if she had lost her mind.

"Finally, her sister, Sweet Amy, heard the noise and ran down the stairs. Mrs. Eva had broken almost every piece of fine china in the house. Amy got mad and told her to shut up and sit down. You should have seen that! The room got holy quiet. We were all shocked that Miss Amy would dare raise her voice to Mrs. Eva.

"At any rate, Mrs. Eva stopped having her fit. Things got quiet for a while. Then Lord! Lord! She started again. Miss Amy sent for Pastor Roberts and Dr. Baker. An hour or so passed and they both arrived, hat in hand. When Mrs. Eva saw that poor doctor, she threw him off the place. She said, 'Baker before I take any of that snake oil you are pedaling, I would rather use slave medicine and die in peace. Git out of my house and off my plantation.'

"Pastor Roberts started quoting scriptures and was looking like he was highly offended that she was cursing so. But that stopped her none! She placed her hands on her huge hips and told poor Pastor Roberts he could take his religion where it was wanted, and that it surely was not wanted on her plantation! Pastor Roberts said he was not going to leave until he had heard from the Lord! She looked him straight in the face, walked across the hall to the desk in the drawing room, pulled out a pistol, and fired two shots, barely missing his head. Well, I guess the Lord spoke to him, cause that old white preacher moved like he had been struck by lightning. Ran out of the house, jumped on his horse, and left.

"Now Mrs. Eva is walking back and forth across the veranda with her pistol in one hand and her shotgun in the other, yelling and talking to herself, shooting that gun at anything in the yard that moves. Thank God she is not a good shot when she is mad and has been drinking. Truly, she has lost her mind!"

"Jenny!" Mrs. Eva yelled. "Jenny! Jenny, tell Old Pete to come here! I want him here right now! I want him to go to town to send a telegram. Tell him to be ready to go when he gets here."

"Yes, ma'am," said Jenny. Quietly, Jenny whispered to Daniel, "Run and get Pete as fast as you can. Hurry! Please hurry! Tell him to bring William with him."

Daniel dashed out the door, racing to the field to get Pete.

Thirty minutes or so passed but finally, Pete arrived. When Mrs. Eva saw Pete, she waved her gun and yelled, "Pete, I want you to go to town and send this telegram. Go to town! Go to the telegraph office and send this message to my daddy in Clear Water, Mississippi. Wait there until you get an answer. If it takes all day and night, wait on the answer. If it takes two to three days, wait on an answer. Do you understand! Drive the wagon and take someone to help you bring back these supplies. Jenny, git him a blanket in case it gets cold tonight. More than likely they will have to stay in town.

"Mrs. Eva, you know we are going to need a pass for night travel or we will have to wait until the next day before we can drive home," said Pete.

"You are right," said Mrs. Eva, and quickly wrote a travel pass for Pete and companions. As soon as Pete got the notes, he ran out the door, jumped in the wagon, and with a crack of the whip above the head of the horses started to town. William held onto the seat to keep from falling off the wagon. Mrs. Eva stood on the veranda watching clouds of dust rise in the air as Pete and William raced to town.

As the wagon passed the bend in the road, Pete stopped the horses, gave William some water to drink, and said, "Boy, can you read this writing?"

"Grand Papa Pete, you know slaves ain't supposed to read nor write," said William. "I have been watching you and Miss Amy. I know you can read. Now it is important for you to read this note! We need to know what is in this paper!"

"All right, said William, "but Miss Amy said if Mrs. Eva knew I could read she would whip me and sell me sure."

"Boy, I ain't going to tell nobody! But we best know what that crazy woman has in these papers."

William began to read the first note. It said:

Telegram

From: **Mrs. Eva Smith**
Cross Junction North Carolina

To: **Colonel James Jethro Gaines**
Clear Water, Mississippi

Papa, my no-good husband went to New Orleans and lost all our money gambling. We are ruined. He is having a slave auction in two weeks to cover his debt. He did not even have the nerve to come home and tell me himself. Percy Scott, a member of your old unit, came fifty miles out of his way to give me the news. Percy said not only will there be a slave auction but he is planning to sell the land, livestock, and furnishings as well. Please come and/or send help. Telegram when you will arrive. All is lost. My slaves have been instructed to wait in town until you send your answer.

Your devoted daughter,

Eva

"Wow said William! Could this be true or just another one of Mrs. Eva's fits?"

"It's true enough if she is sending for her father," said Pete. William folded the note and placed it back in the pouch.

"Now read the next," said Old Grand Papa Pete.

Across the top in large red letters, it said:

Slave Pass

Nov. 23, 1860

My slave Old Grand Papa Pete and companions have my permission to travel on an errand for me. This pass is good until Thanksgiving Day 1860.

      Mrs. Eva Smith, Round Pond Plantation

        Cross Junction, North Carolina

"Who is companions?" asked Pete.

"Me, or anyone traveling with you. So, we have a pass until Thanksgiving Day," said William.

"Thanksgiving is Thursday. We cannot be gone more than four or five days. What does the next note say?"

"It is a list of supplies," said William as he began to read the list. Pete was surprised when William read the supply list. Mrs. Eva wanted lumber, nails, rope, ten boxes of bullets, chains, red and yellow cotton fabric, flour, cornmeal, bacon, sugar, and salt. "What is she planning?"

"My oh my," said William, "they are going to sell us!"

"Yes, it looks that way," William said. "White people shouldn't have the power to just sell us! Why won't God do something to help us? Don't he care about us just a little?"

"He cares," said Pete, "but sometimes a body got to try and help themselves." Grand Papa Pete, sighed, picked up the reins, and slowly started the horses toward town. "When we git to town, do not let anyone know that we know what is in these papers. Mr. Rogers at the store is going to ask me to read the list to him, and I will give him the list upside down. Do not correct me. It is an old trick he uses to see if slaves can read."

In silence, they continued to town. A world of questions ran through William's brain. He knew that being sold was a horrible thing. He wondered where he would be sold. Would he be with his brother, mother, and Grand Papa Pete, or would he be alone?

Tears ran down Old Grand Papa Pete's face. He was remembering how his wife was sold many years ago, and how he never saw her again.

Click, clop, click, clop, went the horses. Birds were chirping in the distance. Wind whirled through the trees. Sadness and despair moved over their bodies.

Old Grand Papa Pete glanced at William, shook his head, and kept driving.

CHAPTER THREE

The Town

Late in the afternoon, they arrived in town. William always liked coming to town. Normally, he and Daniel only came to the outskirts of the town and kept the horses until a race. Once he came to the cotton gin. But today, he was going to be able to see the whole town. He counted ten buildings. He saw the hotel, ladies' store, three dry goods stores, a stable, several saloons, and even a church. He noticed how fine the white people were dressed. The men wore great hats and suits of clothing. The women wore beautiful dresses and carried dainty purses. Some of them carried umbrellas over their head and it was not even raining. But what he noticed most of all was that everyone had shoes—fine shoes and beautiful boots.

Most the slaves he saw looked like him and Grand Papa Pete—raggedy and hungry. He was shocked, as they turned a corner, and he saw a tall black man all dressed up riding on the finest fifteen-hand horse he had ever seen. The man stopped in front of the dry goods store and tipped his hat as they drove by. Who is he? He must be a free man! Oh! To be a free black man. If only William could be free.

Old Grand Papa Pete drove past the stagecoach line down a tree-lined street with big, fine two- and three-story houses. Then he turned down a shabby street with small little shops near the river. He stopped and said, "Boy, do not let on you know what is in these papers. Say nothing unless you are asked. Do not ask any questions. And for God's sake, do not answer any questions about Mrs. Eva!"

After these stern words of warning, Pete climbed down from the wagon and he went into the store at the end of the street. William followed closely behind.

"Good mornin' sir. Mrs. Eva wants to send this message by telegraph."

"She does now!" said the storekeeper angrily. "Did she send any coin?"

"Yes sir! She sent this."

"How much is it, boy?"

"Don't rightly know. It all in here with the paper. She just wants this sent right away, and she said we are to wait here until an answer comes from her papa down in Mississippi."

"Boy, do you know how long that might be?"

"Naw sir," Grand Papa Pete said slowly. "She just said we will have to wait here until a message come back."

Mr. Jones, the storekeeper, slowly took the bag, removed and counted the money, and looked puzzled as he held the note. "Martha, come here quick," he yelled. "Come here quick and read this."

William thought maybe he couldn't read, but surely all white people could read!

Mrs. Martha Jones came to the door and read the note aloud. Then she said, "Send the telegram, Jones. I am going to check the books and see if they owe us money. Now you boys can't wait in the store," she said. "Look at that raggedy child—he doesn't even have shoes! Yaw got to wait outside! You are bad for business," she ordered, holding her nose as she said it.

William and Old Grand Papa Pete started to leave. William could not keep his eyes off the candy jar. "Wait a minute," said Mrs. Jones, sweetly. She walked across the room and placed her hand on the penny candy jar. William looked at the jar with anticipation. Master Ed would sometimes give him a penny candy when he won a horse race. She pulled out a peppermint stick, held it up in the air and said, "Boy, would you like this peppermint?"

"Yeses ma'am!" replied William.

"How is everything at the plantation?"

"We do OK, missus. We got a lot of hard work to do. We still got cotton to pick before winter."

"Pete, are you guys having a good crop this year?"

"Yes ma'am, look like it will be one of the best years we have ever had," he said with pride. "Lots of our cotton has shipped already."

Then she asked William, "How is Mrs. Eva?"

"I live in the barn so I don't know. But she looks fine when I see her on the veranda. She is always dressed in all her fine clothes and jewels," said William.

Martha Jones turned and faced Pete like a madwoman and said, "Do not lie—I know if you lie. How is Mrs. Eva?"

"She seems her normal self, ma'am. Dr. Roberts comes to see Miss Amy now and then but far as I know he ain't never treated Mrs. Eva for nothing. I never known Mrs. Eva to be sick a day since she came to the plantation six years ago. She fine, ma'am."

William and Mrs. Jones made eye contact. She smiled and placed the peppermint stick back in the penny candy jar, tightened the jar lid, and waved her hand for them to get out of the store. William bowed his head, fighting back tears, and began to move to the door.

"Well, I sent the telegram," said Mr. Jones. "It will take a few hours before we get an answer. You boys can't wait in here! You go and wait outside."

"All right," said Pete. "We will wait outside down by the river. When the telegram comes just give us a holler and we will come a-running."

William and old Grand Papa Pete got back in the wagon and drove past the cathouse. William looked up to see that the white women on the upstairs veranda had taken off some of their clothes and were showing their boobs and legs. They were yelling and pulling up their skirts as men went by.

Pete said to William, "Do not look at them, women! That ain't nothing but trouble for a colored man and disease for many white men. Nothing good comes out of a cathouse—no matter how sweet it looks or smells."

William clasped his hands over his eyes. One old prostitute saw him and laughed until she almost fell over the veranda.

William saw a steamboat in the river. The boat could take passengers up and down the river, north or south.

"Which way is north?" he asked "I would like to go north and be free."

"Hush boy, do not let anyone hear you say that," said Old Pete quietly. "But north is that way. Moss always grows on the north side of the tree. Ain't nothing wrong about wanting to be free. On a bright night, the big dipper will lead the way north.

"We will camp here in these woods. I am going to cool down the horses and water them at the river. Go and get firewood and look for nuts or anything we may eat. Set a snare for a rabbit. And when it gets a little later, maybe we can catch a fish or two. If you find horse chestnut seeds or an eagle fern plant, bring them so we can have some soap with which to wash. You and I both could stand a good washing. I will meet you here in an hour or two."

They waited all afternoon, but not a word came. Pete told William to crack the horse chestnut seeds, place them in a small pan of water, and wash up. William was surprised to see how many soap bubbles they made. Then, William washed his hands. They washed their face and feet as well.

"Did you find any eagle fern?"

"Yes, I did," said William.

"Go and bring it here. After supper, I will show you how to make enough soap to wash our clothes and bathe."

When it was almost time for the store to close, Pete went to the telegraph office and asked if there was a message from Mrs. Eva's papa.

"No answer," said Mr. Jones. "Look like you and that boy will have to spend the night in the open. It looks like rain. You best take shelter for the night. Stay away from town; some riffraff has been coming in lately causing trouble for poor whites and niggers alike. Stay close to the river and out of sight. Keep a dark camp tonight."

"You expecting trouble, sir?"

"Yes, I am, Pete. Times are changing and it ain't safe for a poor man and niggers." Pete went back to the little camp and told William they would be staying the night. He moved the wagon to a little holler that could not be seen from the road. He dug two holes; one was six feet long and the other about four feet. Each hole was just six to twelve inches deep. Next, he drove the wagon over the holes, cut evergreen branches, and covered the wagon, leaving the south side open. They built a small, smokeless fire, and he placed large rocks in the fire and cooked the rabbit William caught. After supper, Pete took the hot stones and placed them in the holes and covered the holes with the soil and evergreen branches.

"This is a ground bed," he said. It will keep you warm. Go to sleep now. I will keep watch."

William took some old feed bags that were in the wagon and covered the ground bed so it would be more comfortable lying on the evergreen branches. Then he placed one bag over himself like a blanket. Soon he felt the warmth from the rocks below and before he knew it, he was asleep.

Pete placed some of the eagle fern in a bucket of water. He thought by morning they should have enough soapy water to wash their clothes. Old Grand Papa Pete covered himself with the blanket Jenny had placed on the wagon and kept watch near a tree close to the wagon. It was Wednesday night, yet he could hear laughter and frolicking coming from the cathouse and the saloons. Every now and then he would hear gunshots. Plantation owners, gamblers, town people, and farmers were in town celebrating their harvest, kicking up their heels and having a good time.

About nine o'clock the moon came out and he could see the North Star. He looked at the star and thought about running to freedom land. Oh! how wonderful it would be to be free. He thought of the old African saying: "If you want to go fast, go alone. If you want to go far, go together."

Pete took out his knife and made a spear from one of two straight oak limbs he had hidden in the wagon. Then he placed the spear on the ground beside him. He remembered that his father had made spears in Africa. He remembered being free. That was so very long ago. People called him old Grand Papa Pete, but he was not quite forty-five years old.

He carved a round, ball on the end of the other oak limb. White people would be upset if they saw the spear but they would think nothing of an old man using a walking stick. But it wasn't a walking stick, it was a killing club. These were the only weapons they had for protection, and he knew there were more things to worry about than wild animals.

At about 2:00 a.m. it began to rain slightly. By 3:00 a.m. it was a downpour. The temperature dropped and it got very cold. Pete crawled under the wagon and laid on the bed he had made. He could feel the warmth from the stones in the ground on his back and he was grateful for this warm, dry place to sleep. He looked at William and prayed that God would keep them safe—and if he had a mind to set them free! And he ended his prayer as he did every night by saying, "Lord, I need you!"

CHAPTER FOUR

Winds of Hope

At daylight, Pete checked the horses and led them to the river to drink. He checked his fish traps and found that he had caught enough fish to eat and extra to sell. He wanted very much to get a penny to buy a piece of candy for William. It was so cruel how Mrs. Martha Jones teased the boy with the candy.

He made breakfast for him and William and walked toward town to see if there was an answer to the telegram. As he walked past the cathouse, the Negro cook saw him and said, "I give you a fair trade for some of those fish."

"OK," said Pete, "what do you have in mind?"

"Looks like you could use a coat or some other clothes or some shoes, maybe a pair of socks for that boy I saw you with yesterday. It is going to be a very cold winter. Come to the backyard and let's see if we can make a trade."

Pete eyed the woman. She had a kind face, and judging from her size she loved her cooking.

"Here!" said Pete. "You take the fishes and you can give me whatever clothes and shoes you see fit. The boy ain't never had shoes. Most winter, he and his brother just have rags to cover their feet and bodies. I must go to the telegraph office. Be back directly."

"Be careful!" said the cook. "Last night there was talk of war coming to the south soon— war that may free a Negro man. Many of the whites at the cathouse last night said they rather see a dead nigger than a free nigger."

"Why are so many people in town?" asked Pete.

"The steamboat is being repaired. They will be leaving on Friday, after Thanksgiving."

"Did you hear any other news?" asked Pete.

"Oh! My Lord, yes! Banker Jefferson was in with my girl, Rachel, and he said a large plantation was going to need to have a slave auction in a couple of weeks and they would have to sell most of everything! The banker was planning to buy the land for cheap. You hear anything about that?" she asked.

"No, I ain't," said Pete. "I must be going now. I need to be there when the telegraph office opens."

So, the banker knows about the slave auction, Peter thought. If he had Daniel with him, he, Daniel, and William would run for freedom! Sold like a pig or horse. "Lord God! Lord God!" he said under his breath.

Within a few minutes he was at Mr. Jones's place.

"Good morning," said Pete.

"No news yet, Pete. It sure is cold today."

"Yas sir it is. I will check back later."

Pete walked past Mr. Jones's store and stopped at the general store of Mr. Gamble. "Morning sir, I have a list from Mrs. Eva. Could I pick this up later? I am waiting on a telegram for Mrs. Eva. I need to pick up these things after the telegram comes. Might be a day or so."

Mr. Gamble took the note, read it, and said, "I think I have most of this."

"OK sir, I am waiting on a message for Mrs. Eva. I will be back to pick up the things on the list as soon as I get that telegram message."

"Alright, just bring someone to help you load your wagon," Mr. Gamble said, then asked, "Boy, how is y'all's cotton crop this year?"

"Sir it has been powerful good. Best year ever! We still have cotton in the fields and about six hundred more bales to bring to town. They will have picked everything by Thanksgiving or soon after."

"Good to hear," he said. "Come on by when you are ready and get those things for Mrs. Eva."

"Yes, sir I will," said Pete.

Pete turned and began to walk back to the river. When he came to the cathouse he went to the back and knocked on the door. The negro cook said in a sexy voice, "Hey, hey, Mr. Pete. Here is a package for you. The ladies loved your fish and here are bits of clothing men have left here over the years. They gave more things than usual because Martha Sue saw your little man."

"William, you mean."

"Yes, William stole her heart when he put both of his hands over his eyes to keep from seeing her standing half-naked on the veranda. She even sent a bit of candy for him."

"You know your boy could pass for white," she went on. "He is a handsome little boy. He is tall, has a broad chin and well-shaped nose, hazel eyes, and big shoulders. I bet he will grow to be over six feet, like you. He's goanna a be a knockout with that vanilla skin, reddish brown hair, good looks, and smile that can melt ice. Shame he is a slave. If a child like that could get north no one would ever guest he was not a white man. Then he could be free! Well, as I was saying, Mr. Pete, here is the package for you."

"Thank you," said Pete.

"If you catch any more fish before you have to go home bring them by."

"OK, I will," he said.

"By the way, Pete, there is some more news. It seems some woman was foolish enough to trust her husband with her money and now he has gone to New Orleans and lost all that money and the bank is going to take her land if she can't pay the mortgage. Horrible, horrible! You hear anything about that?"

"No, said Pete, "not a thang."

"I wish I could remember the name of the man they were talking about. My mind ain't what it used to be."

"Thanks for the clothing," said Pete. "Ma'am, I got to go."

"Wait! Here are some biscuits and such for you and the boy. Are you sure I can't do anything else for you, Mr. Pete?" she said in a sexy voice as she moved her hips back and forth and pulled her skirt up a little. You sure are a fine, fine, good-looking man—your big shoulders, coffee-colored skin. You must be over six feet tall or more. Mr. Pete, you make me think of sinful things!"

Nervously Pete said, "Thank you, ma'am, but I got to be going. Some other time maybe!" Pete smiled and tipped his hat as he left.

At the campsite William was waiting. His eyes were big and wide open. Pete could see he had been crying.

"What's wrong?" asked Pete.

"You were gone so long I thought you had left me!"

"No, never," said Pete. "I thought about running for freedom but I wouldn't leave you, your brother, or your mom. If I take the freedom road, we will go as a family."

Pete pulled out the little bundle with food and shared it with William. William smacked his lips and tapped his foot and said, "This food is delicious!" Finally, he asked, "What is in the big bundle?"

"Let's see. I traded our fish for this bundle of rags. Maybe we will not be so cold this winter." When they opened the bundle, they found a small coat, sweater, and pants just William's size, along with another outfit that would fit Daniel with a funny little coat called a poncho. Then Pete found a warm blue woolen scarf and a long blue sweater. He wrapped the scarf around his neck and put on the sweater. At the very bottom of the bag there were two pairs of old, rundown shoes, mix-matched socks and two peppermint candy sticks. William held up the shoes and began to dance all around. It did not bother him that they were too big and had holes in their bottoms. Let's save the candy for Christmas, said William. Old Pete nodded his head and told William to bring him the clothes. He put mud on the clothes and hung them by the fire to dry.

"Why did you put mud on our clothes?"

"Cause, we can't go back with new clothes. That will certainly set off Mrs. Eva—and she's crazy enough already."

William nodded his head in agreement.

"Go and look for some of those medicinal herbs by the river. Gather what you can find. Look and see if we caught a rabbit and reset the snare if we have. I am going to water and feed the horses. Be back in an hour or so."

Pete walked down to the river to water the horses. On the way back from the river, he met Mr. George.

"Hey, boy," he said. "Mr. Jones said if I was to see you down at the river to tell you to come quickly to the store—to bring your wagon and all."

Pete hurried up the hill, hitched the team of horses, and yelled for William.

"I is a coming, I is a coming!" yelled William. "We got us a rabbit and I found an asafetida bush."

"Good God almighty!" said Pete. "What a streak of luck! Get as many leaves as you can from the bush. Skin that rabbit quick! Save the skin and we will tan it to put in those shoes. Put that rabbit and its skin in this bag and place it under the wagon seat, then run to the fish trap and see if we caught anything. Fish or no fish be sure to bring me my trap. And hurry! We got to go. Telegram's here."

William skinned the rabbit, placed it under the wagon seat, and then he ran to check the fish trap. He pulled up the trap to find four very large catfish. They were almost too heavy for him to carry. When Pete saw what he had, he ran to meet him.

"Man look at those fish!" he declared. "What a beautiful sight! Put these fish in the old cook pot, place them under the seat, and cover the pot with sacks. If Mr. Jones sees them, he be wanting to take them all."

Next, they cleaned up the camp and headed for town. When they passed the cathouse Pete stopped, took two of the catfish, ran to the back door, and left the fish for the cook. She gave him a big hug and smiled.

"I got to go," he said, "Thank you for them shoes. Would you have a bit of salt, ma'am?"

"Yes, we do. I don't think it would be missed if I gave you some."

She ran in the house and returned with a small bag of salt for Pete. She kissed him on the cheek. He held her in his arms, rubbed his hands down her back, and across her hips, returned the kiss, and said goodbye. The cook smiled and said, "Next time Mr. Pete!"

Pete hopped back onto the wagon and pulled away, stopping in front of the telegraph office. He hurried out of the wagon.

"Hi, Mr. Jones. Mr. George told me you wanted me to come."

"Yes, yes!" said Jones. "Here is the message. Take it to Mrs. Eva as soon as you can."

"Will do, sir. Just got to stop and pick up things Mrs. Eva ordered from Gamble's store."

"Hmm!" he said. "Hurry, then—ain't safe for you to travel at night."

This was the second time Mr. Jones had warned him about traveling at night. Something must be up. What was it? wondered Pete. Mr. Jones usually wasn't very friendly.

"Yes, sir," said Pete. He took the telegram and placed it in a bag and tied it around his waist. Next, he went to Gamble's store.

"Mr. Gamble, I am here to fetch those things for Mrs. Eva."

"Fine, fine," he said. "Pull your wagon around back and we will get it loaded. My man Sam is here and he will help you."

Sam and Pete loaded the wagon, neither man saying a word. Finally, Sam said, "Walk with me to the well, Pete, and help me get some water."

"All right," said Pete.

When they got to the well Sam said, "I want to tell you something but I did not want Mr. Gamble or Mrs. Gamble to hear. I just came back on the riverboat with Mr. Gamble two days ago with supplies for the winter. When we docked in Mobile, I heard folks talking about a Mr. Smith that went to New Orleans and lost all his money and gambled away part of his land trying to get back some of the money he lost. The gamblers told him they did not want land in Carolina, but if he had slaves, he could sell them, settle his debt, and keep the land. That stupid man agreed to do so, I am told. You cannot raise cotton nor tobacco without slaves. Now some poor Negro children will be sold before Christmas. A slave auction is a misery for all. Some of the worst people show up. I did not think any more of it until Mr. Jones came by last night and told Mr. Gamble about Mrs. Eva's telegram. Then I remembered her name is Eva Smith. The telegram from her father arrived yesterday, but for some reason they didn't tell you until today. They are planning something.

"Do you know what is in the telegram?" asked Pete.

"There were two telegrams yesterday," Sam said. "Telegram one said Ed Smith lost all of Mrs. Eva's money gambling and speculating. He must raise money to prevent foreclosure. He has decided to hold an auction of slaves, livestock, and furnishings.

"Do you know who sent that telegram?" Pete asked.

"No, I was listening through a crack in the window," Sam said. "In telegram two, Mrs. Eva asked her papa to come and help her. Her papa sent back a telegram and said he could not come but he would send some men to help her. They will be here a few days after Thanksgiving. Sorry to give you such bad news. Mr. George, Mr. Jones, and Mr. Gamble are trying to see how they can be sure they get the monies owed them by Master Ed and become rich off of the Smith Plantation."

"Hey! What you boys talking about?" yelled Mr. Gamble.

"Nothing sir," said Sam, "just passing the time."

"Except I was offering Sam some of the fish I caught this morning," replied Pete.

"Fish you say! Come back to the house and let me see."

Pete went to the wagon and took out one of the fish.

"Now that is a big catfish—looks like a twenty-pounder." Mr. Gamble took a meat cleaver from the wall off the porch and cut off the head and tail of the fish. "Here!" he said. "Sam, you can have the fish's head. Pete, you and the boy can have the tail. Me and the Mrs. gonna eat the rest. We are gonna have a fine, fine supper tonight. You boys don't mind, do you?" he said with a crooked smile, as if they had a choice. "You boys would get sick eating this fine fish—tear your stomach right up. Mmm what a mighty fine fish it is," said Mr. Gamble as he went back into the store and called his wife. Sam's face fell. Pete lowered his eyes. William looked around the wagon but said nothing.

Sam said, "Pete, I am sorry about your fish. They are always listening and do not want us to have nothing, not even the food we find for ourselves."

"Not a problem," said Pete. "Here is some asafetida. Dry the leaves and make tea—it will keep you strong. What is the big pole and chain for?"

"Mr. George had it put in while I was away. At night he chains me to that pole so I can't run away. The chain is barely long enough for me to go into the slave hut."

"Have you heard any more news?" Pete asked.

"The only thing I heard on the river was talk of war! War between the north and south. The southerners are getting ready to beat the Yankees. They think there will be a war for sure after Christmas and they will be victorious and back home by the fall."

"Thank you," said Pete. "We must be on our way."

"Do not travel at night," warned Sam. "And do not use the river road to go home.

Sometimes people who leave the Gamble store with lots of goods get robbed on their way home, and I restock the very same thing I help them load the day before. You and this boy would be easy picking. Go back to the plantation via the old mining road. It will take a little longer but it is a lot safer. Do not travel at night. When you stop, hide the wagon and the horses."

"Bye Sam," said Pete. "Hope to see you when this trouble is over."

"Stay alive," said Sam. "Just try to stay alive! And so will I."

CHAPTER FIVE

Decisions

Pete and William rode past the big houses in the small town and headed west toward home. After a few miles William said, "I did not talk to anyone like you said while we were in town but I have a few questions."

"Questions!"

"Yes sir. Why didn't you tell, that lady about Mrs. Eva? Even when she said, 'Do not lie to me—I will know if you lie to me.'"

Pete laughed.

"I did not lie to her. I said Mrs. Eva was her usual self. Now, was that not the truth?" William giggled. "There was no need for me to tell her how Mrs. Eva was acting. Telling her would only cause me trouble. She had read the telegram message that Mrs. Eva sent her Pa and just wanted more information. It was best that we acted as if all was normal. If she wanted to find out the truth then she could talk to Pastor Roberts or Doc Baker. Maybe she will, but I doubt it. She is a poor merchant's wife in this community and she will not openly ask about a woman above her station."

"Oh!" said William. William remembered just because someone asked a question did not mean you had to answer it or tell them all you know.

"That lady was trying to see what we knew. That is why she acted as if she was going to give you that peppermint stick. Take out the telegram. Can you read it?"

"I can't open the envelope. It's glued shut," said William.

"That's too bad," said Pete.

"While you and Sam were loading the wagon, that black woman, the cook who gave us the clothes, came by and gave me this little bag. She said to hide it and not open it until we were way out of town. So, I put it in my coat."

"OK, let's see. Mmm that smells like a good biscuit," said Pete. William looked at the paper the biscuit was wrapped in and began to cry. "Boy, what's wrong with you! Say something, boy! Give me that biscuit! What's wrong! Cat got your tongue?"

"It's the paper the biscuit is wrapped in."

"All I see is a white paper."

"Yes sir, there is white paper on one side but the other side it says: 'Slave Auction.' " Pete stopped the horses and drove them to the side of the road.

"William," he said, "Take your time and read that paper."

William held up the flyer and read each word slowly.

Slave Auction
Round Pond Plantation
Cross Junction, North Carolina
Mr. Ed Smith, Owner

For Sale
200 Slaves: Men, women, and children
Livestock
Household furnishings
December 15, 1860

"Lord! Lord! We are all going to be sold. Ain't more than two hundred people on the place. I had hoped he would only have to sell a few, but he is planning to sell everyone! Read that note again, William."

William did as he was told and read the flyer a second time. Pete took the flyer from William. He stepped down from the wagon and stared at it in disbelief. Then he knelt down, hit the two flint rocks together, started a fire, and burned the paper. After a long while, he got back on the wagon and continued down the road in silence.

Finally, he said, "When we get back to the plantation, tell no one about the flyer. We are going to go home via the mining road and I am going to try to teach you how to survive. If we are not sold together, you must survive! You must live! Stay close to your brother. If your mama and brother were here, we would run north. Be relentless about your desire to be free! You are eleven, soon to be twelve years old. Today you must become a man!"

He handed William a bag and continued, "Here is my medicine bag. People call me a slave doctor. I want you to look at these leaves and roots and remember how they are used. When a slave becomes sick most masters do not spent money on a doctor. They will sometime give a slave the same medicine they give a horse or cow but we ain't livestock. This medicine has been passed down from my grandmother who brought knowledge of similar medicine from across the ocean—a place called Africa. She was not always a slave. Once she was an African princess."

"Are you sure?" asked William.

"Yes, it is true," said Pete. "We do not have a lot of time. You must remember what I'm gonna tell you. We will do this in groups of five. When you know those five, we will go to the next five, and so on until you know the entire list:

"Number one: sassafras root tea. It cleans the blood. Number two: pokeweed or poke salad. It is a poison, and it can cause sickness or death or be eaten for food. Number three: jimsonweed tea—use it for rheumatism. Number four: horse chestnut leaf tea—for asthma. Number five: horse chestnut seeds—soap.

"Now for the next group. Number six: mint or cow chip tea is for constipation. Number seven: asafetida or devil dung—use it to cure most anything. Number eight: garlic—wards off disease. Eat it whenever you can. Number nine: mustard plaster—pneumonia. Take one part ground mustard seed and four parts wheat flour. Mix and place on the chest for fifteen to thirty minutes—not any longer or it will burn your skin. Number ten: rue—antidote for poison and plagues and it can cause pregnant women to bleed and lose their babies.

"Next is number eleven: boneset—for fever. Number twelve: sage—treats colic in children, and you can gargle to cure a sore throat. Number thirteen: pennyroyal—treats colds, fever, headaches, or toothaches. Number fourteen: catnip—sleep. Number fifteen: peppermint or spearmint—relieves indigestion, stomach cramps, nausea.

"Now for the next five. Number sixteen: horehound—sore throat, cough, and cold symptoms. Number seventeen: Sampson's snakeroot—snake bite and other poisons. Number eighteen: peach tree leaves—rid a body of worms, morning sickness, and malaria, and they can be used as a poison. Number nineteen: cherry or dogwood—chills or fever. Number twenty: cotton, for when a woman does not want a child. But she must chew on it every day.

"And last but not least, number twenty-one: laurel—death—seed, leaves, or the roots. Four seeds can kill a toddler.

"Sometimes the white folks will provide castor oil, quinine, or turpentine for slaves. But most of the time they do not think we should be treated with the same medicine they treat themselves. It is up to us to stay healthy and alive."

"I know most of these plants you are talking about by sight," said William. "But I will have to learn what they are used for."

"That is fine," said Old Grand Papa Pete. "The way I figure it, we got a week before they start getting ready for the auction."

William pulled out each herb in the first group one by one and repeated its uses over and over again until Old Pete was satisfied that William could remember the plant and its uses.

"Mighty fine," said Grand Papa Pete, "mighty fine. Here are the next five. We will do as before."

This continued until William knew the twenty-one plants and their uses.

"Now repeat what I told you."

"I wish I could write this down."

"You can write, boy?"

"Yes," said William. "Reading and writing sort of go together."

"Never let anyone know you can write and read. If the white folks find out you can do either they will hurt or kill you to keep you from teaching others."

For the next few hours, Pete made William recite the slave medical remedies. When they got to the river, William cleaned the fish. Pete watered the horses and drove the team of horses and wagon down the dry creek bed.

"Why are we not going straight?" asked William.

"I am going to take Sam's advice and go home via the mining road. But we are going to hide our tracks so no one will know we left the road here. It is getting late and we will not be able to get home tonight. We must find a safe place to hide."

They drove down the dry creek bed for a few miles and then went up a hill to the mine road. Old Pete jumped off the wagon, took some brush and wiped out their tracks, and continued down the road. Finally, he stopped and hid the wagon and horses.

"We will leave early in the morning," he said. "Sorry we cannot have a fire. But I will show you how to cure a rabbit's hide. We can place the hide in those holey shoes."

"OK," said William.

"Here are the steps. We will do this first rabbit skin together and then you will do the next one by yourself. Here is the whole process:

"One: peel the skin off the rabbit.

"Two: take all of flesh of the skin. Now, this step takes time.

"Three: rub salt in the skin. Let the salt stay on the skin about three to four hours, scrape the salt off, then put on the next layer of salt and let it sit for twelve to twenty-four hours.

"Four: stretch the hide and let it dry two to four days.

"Five: scrape the salt and soak it in fresh warm water. Do not remove the skin until it is nice and soft.

"Six: let the skin dry.

"Now go get that rabbit skin and let's get started."

The next morning when William awoke, Old Grand Papa Pete had hitched the horses to the wagon and was ready to go.

"Nothing to eat this morning?" asked William.

"Sorry, it ain't safe to make a fire. Look for a persimmon tree or nut trees, like pecan, walnut, or acorn."

"Maybe we can find something to eat," said William.

"Stop thinking about eating. Look and see if you see any of the plants we talked about last night. Act as if we are playing a game."

"OK," said William, "that will be a good game. I like games."

About midmorning, William yelled, "Stop the wagon! There is a pecan tree and persimmon tree."

Old Pete stopped the wagon.

"These horses need a rest," he said. "Go and gather as much as you can. You must hurry. We need to get back as soon as we can."

William ran and gathered pecans and several persimmons. He found two sage bushes and placed them in the bag. When he saw Old Grand Papa Pete waving, he ran back to the wagon. He gave Pete one of the persimmons.

"Look what I found," said William.

"Do you know what that is?" asked Pete.

"Yes, I do. This is sage," he said proudly.

"What do you use it for?"

"Fever, colic, and sore throat—and Aunty Jenny likes to cook with it. And I like to eat her cooking."

They both gave a small laugh.

It began to get colder. Pete told William to put on all the clothes.

"Even the clothes for Daniel?"

"Yes," said Pete. "Make sure your old clothes are on top."

Soon they rounded the bend and were ready to reconnect to the river road. Just before they came to the intersection, they heard horses and many men laughing and firing guns. Pete stopped the wagon and pulled into a small grove of oak trees. He signaled William to be quiet. They could hear a lot of yelling and fighting, but could not see what was happening. Finally, Pete climbed up the bluff so he could see what was happening down below.

The well-dressed black man, the free black man they had seen in town, had been stripped of his fine clothes. One man had his horse, the other had taken his saddle and gun. One of the white men was angry because they had killed the black man when they hit him over the head.

"We could have sold him back into slavery. We could have gotten two thousand or more for him!" one shouted. "But you had to kill him."

The men rolled the black man's body into a ditch by the river, climbed on their horses, and rode east toward the Anderson Plantation. Pete did not recognize any of the men, but he would remember that horse anywhere. What a fine stallion!

Pete and William stayed in their hiding spot for another hour. Then Pete drove the team down from the mining road to the river road junction. When he got to the ditch, he got down from the wagon and checked to see if the man was truly dead. He rolled the man, over put his ear to the man's heart, and he heard a weak *boom, boom*. This poor man was alive. Alive! But where could they take him? What would be safe?

Pete put the man in the wagon, covered him with a quilt, and left the junction in the road as quickly as possible. The black man began to moan, but he was still unconscious. They moved down the river road and came to Cooper's Crossing. Pete turned left and headed up the road to old Ms. Cooper's home. Ms. Cooper was a tiny old white woman who lived by herself. She was a wise, kind woman who went around the county preaching. It was said she was a part of the underground railroad, but Pete did not know that for sure. Maybe she would help the man or maybe not. He was taking a big chance to ask her, but his choices were few.

When they reached the house the man was barely conscious, and he was complaining of a huge headache.

"Wait here!" said Pete.

He knocked on the door and waited. After several minutes Ms. Cooper came to the door.

"Why it is you, Old Grand Papa Pete. It takes me some while to come to the door these days. What brings you here?"

"I found a man in a ditch by the road. He had been left for dead. He needs some help!

Would you help him?"

"Why don't you take him to y'all's place?"

"I can't. He is a freed black man. He was robbed by someone going toward the Anderson's Place. If I take him to Round Pond Plantation with us, he would lose his freedom and be a slave again. At the very least, please let him stay here a few hours and give him some clothes."

When she heard what Pete had said she came out of her door, sat down on the porch, and thought for a long while. Then she said, "Take him to the barn. I will see if I can find passage for him on the next train."

"Train? What train, Ms. Cooper?"

"Never you mind. We should have one leaving in five days. You and yours may want to ride on the train someday. Just listen for the song "Steal Away Home" and watch for the traveler quilt hanging on my fence."

Pete then understood what she meant, the underground railroad, but said nothing. He wondered if old age had begun to affect her mind. Then he said, "Thank you," and took the man to the barn.

"My name is Pete Smith and this is William," he said to the man. "You were robbed and left for dead. I got to leave you here with Ms. Cooper. She 'bout the only decent white person in this area—the only chance you have. Can't take you with me causes we is slaves. She will try to get you out on the next underground railway train. But if I was you, I would leave North Carolina as soon as I could. I can't stay here with you any longer—I am overdue at the plantation. She is a good old white woman, but her mind is foggy at times."

"Thank you," said the man. "My name is Clifford Burns. If I make it, you can find me in Brownville, Tennessee. Many thanks. I will never forget this! My head is hurting something powerful. They really worked me over."

"Here is some pennyroyal," said Pete. "It helps get rid of headaches and fever. All I have to give you is a few pecans and a persimmon or two we found on the road."

"Why did they rob you?" asked William.

"They wanted the horse and to sell me back into slavery. That horse is a prime Arabian stallion. I trained him from a pony myself. He is worth a great deal of money. But they robbed me because they could and if I complained to the sheriff nothing would be done about it. As long as they think I am dead I got a chance."

Old Pete and William turn the wagon around and headed toward the plantation. Pete prayed that the man would survive and see his Tennessee.

CHAPTER SIX

Strange Things

Pete and William were silent as they rode toward Round Pond Plantation. Suddenly, William yelled, "What's that in the tree line?" William saw what he thought was a half-human, half-demon running through the trees. "Is it a haint?" He moved closer to Pete in sheer horror.

The thing was yelling, talking to air or something. William could not see. It was putting mud and cow dung in its hair and on its body. Then it began to wave its arms all around, howling and chanting. William had never heard such a pitiful, sorrowful sound.

As they came closer, William asked again, "What is that?"

"It is not a what. It is a who," said Old Pete. "That poor thing once was the prettiest-looking woman on this plantation."

"That poor thang is Mary? She is crazy! Stone crazy!" said William.

"Yes, she is that all right," said Pete. "Once she was a tall, well-shaped Quadroon girl who fell in love with Master Ed and bore him a child. That baby was her pride and joy. Master Ed was always spending time at her cabin. This was after he married Mrs. Eva. Mrs. Eva hated Mary and warned Master Smith to stay away from her and that little boy. But he didn't. One day in a fit of rage Mrs. Eva drowned the child in the washtub, and Mary lost her mind. That was nearly five years ago. I am surprised she is still alive!

"After her baby died, she tried to burn down the Big House and ran off into the woods. They tried to find her for days. Master even hired that Indian Cherokee Big Knife with his dogs to track her. But she could not be found. Big Knife said his dogs could not pick up her scent 'causes she had covered herself with mud and cow dung. Winter came and went. Finally, in the spring they found her clothes by the river. Most folks thought she had jumped into the river and drowned or had been kilt by some animal. Look at the poor thang! Poor Miss Mary!"

They watch her for a moment along the tree line. Then in an instant she was gone, back into the thick forest. The horses were rattled, frightened, and tried to bolt. But Pete pulled back on the reins and got them under control. He talked to the horses until they settled down. He slowed their pace to little more than a walk and proceeded down the road.

Pete wanted to enjoy these last moments of freedom. Neither he nor William said a word. The sadness they felt as they returned to the plantation, Mrs. Evil Eva, and the knowledge that everyone was to be sold at a slave auction was almost unbearable.

They arrived at the driveway to the Big House about 2:30 p.m. Pete let out a big *ghee gee* yell to announce that he and William were back.

He drove up to the Veranda of the Big House where Mrs. Eva was waiting. Pete jumped off the wagon, ran, and gave her the telegram. She ripped open the seal, read it, and gave it to her sister Miss Amy.

"Thank you, Pete," said Miss Amy. "Look like you made good time. Mr. Jones did not think you would have gotten here before nightfall. Take that wagon around back and unload it. Then go to the barn and bring me those large crates stored on the upper floor."

"How many, ma'am?"

"Oh, I think three will do."

"Right away ma'am!"

Pete ran back to the wagon and drove it around back.

"William, go and tell Frank to come and help me unload this wagon. You are too small to do it. Then stay in the barn until I come," said Old Grand Papa Pete.

"Aunty Jenny, we brought you a present," William said with a huge grin.

"Present! God almighty! What in the world could it be?"

"Sage, good-smelling sage, and I left the root on it so you could keep it growing." William took the sage from his knapsack and gave it to Aunty Jenny. She hugged him, brushing back tears.

"Run on and get Frank, William. Tell him to hurry!" William ran happily toward the barn.

"How have things been?" asked Grand Papa Pete.

"Bad, really bad," said Jenny. "Mrs. Eva has been out of her mind. She has made us wash and iron everything in the place. She is finding jobs for people that don't even need doing. She keeps the field hands out picking cotton from sunup to past dark and she has cut the food ration.

"Mrs. Eva went to the slave quarters with Overseer Jackson and wrote down the names of each slave, and what they did—like if they were cottonfield hands or worked in the tobacco barn or such. She even went into the fields and counted all the horses and cows. She didn't realize that half of the livestock was in the lower pastures until Overseer Jackson told her. She hired four extra men to monitor the plantation at night. No one is allowed out after the big bell rings.

"Every morning I have been making her some peppermint tea to calm her nerves. Filling the house with lavender oil hoping it will help her mood. And each night I been slipping catnip in her tea to help her sleep. But she still wakes in the middle of the night cursing and screaming what a low life Master Smith is and how she is going to get her revenge. Her mood changes with the wind. I keep wondering if she gone completely—"

"Jenny! Jenny!" yelled Mrs. Eva. "Come here! Come here quick! Tell those boys to hurry! We got a lot to do."

Jenny ran toward the parlor to attend to Mrs. Eva without finishing her statement. There was no need; Pete knew what was wrong with Mrs. Eva. And he knew she was making a list of things on the plantation she could sell, from humans to hogs.

Old Grand Papa Pete and Frank began to unload the wagon. Miss Amy was there supervising their every move, instructing where she wanted each item placed. Finally, they came to the last box. It was long and heavy. As they began to lift it, the top came off and they saw brand new repeating rifles and ammunition and several large hog-killing knives. Neither man said a word. They both look to see if Miss Amy had noticed. Thankfully, she was distracted by her dog Max. So, they secured the top back on the box and brought the box out of the wagon. When Miss Amy saw the box, she said, "Just the one I have been looking for. Take that box upstairs to the drawing room."

The men looked at each other and did as they were told. They noticed a note on the box but neither man could read it. Pete promised himself he was gonna learn to read come hell or high water.

"Now go get my boxes!" said Miss Amy.

Pete took the empty wagon back to the barn and loaded three large crates for Mrs. Eva.

When he and Frank returned to the Big House she asked, "Pete what did you see in town?"

"Lots of people are celebrating ma'am and a riverboat needing repairs. The boat was supposed to be fixed and on its way by Friday or Saturday morning at the latest."

"Oh!" she said. "If the riverboat left on Friday, when would it get to its next stop upriver?"

"Hmm, the next stop is Camden," Pete said slowly. "It will probably be there in two days or so. It will take a day or more to reload the cotton after the boat is repaired. So that riverboat should be leaving Camden Monday or Tuesday morning at the latest. But there will be another boat going upriver Thursday, ma'am cause, it is the fourth Thursday in the month. Anyway, you look at it some boat is leaving Camden next Tuesday or Thursday going upriver, close as I can figure."

"Pete, what's closer to this plantation, Cross Junction or Camden?"

"Camden, ma'am."

"Why do we always go to Cross Junction?"

"Ma'am I do not know. I thought you liked the shops and the people. Ain't but one or two stores in Camden—no churches, hotels, or places to eat. Just Mr. Harry Burns' cotton gin and his store. Sometimes he lets travelers sleep in his backrooms. Don't you remember him, ma'am? Tall skinny man with freckles. Came here last Christmas for your big party."

Abruptly she said, "Place the crates in the dining room, Pete."

"Yes ma'am," he said. He thought maybe their talk had gotten too friendly or he had said to much. Dangerous grounds! Dangerous grounds. Alarm bells went off in his head. She was acting like a cornered animal thinking about charging—or, how to get out of a cage but unable to figure out which way to go.

Then, she asked, "Pete how many hours will it take to go to Camden? What's the quickest way?"

"About five to six hours, ma'am if we go across the mountain on horseback. If you use the Camden road it will take almost a day with a wagon."

"Why does it take so long on the river?"

"Well ma'am, they can't travel that part of the river at night. There are a lot of twists and turns plus sand traps, which makes the river travel from Cross Junction to Camden three times as long. But after that the river is a lot faster than land."

"Thanks, Pete," she said. "Good day! Come here at daylight tomorrow morning." Pete said, "Yes ma'am," and he left the room. But as he left, he wondered what crazy things were going on in her head. She was plotting something. And if she was caught by Master Ed, he would beat her for sure and whip the slaves who helped her.

CHAPTER SEVEN

Family Ties

Daniel and William were eagerly waiting for Old Grand Papa Pete. The barn had been bursting at the seams with people. The white overseer, Graves, was there checking all the horses and stalls. The new man, Flint Carter, even went into Old Grand Papa Pete's room and searched the mattress of straw and looked in all the jars and jugs. He threw things everywhere.

"Tell Pete I am sorry," said Carter, "Mrs. Eva's ordered this."

"I told you Old Pete did not have weapons stored away in his room," said Graves.

"Who is that man with Mr. Graves?" asked William in a whisper.

"I don't really know," Daniel said softly. "His name is Carter. They have been searching every cabin on the place. When they find a knife or anything sharp, they take it and place it in a large basket in the Big House kitchen. They even took the hay forks and sugarcane machetes.

They are expecting something to happen—or something has happened and we do not know it yet."

Finally, Mr. Graves and the stranger Carter left the barn. It was almost night fall.

"At last, we can talk," said Daniel. "How did you like the trip into town? What did you learn?"

"A lot," said William. "Do you know just because a white woman says she can do something does not mean she can!"

"I knew that already," says Daniel.

"Well, I didn't," said William. "Mrs. Jones from the store wanted to know about Mrs. Eva. I said she looked OK to me when I saw her on the veranda. Then she spun around to Old Grand Papa Pete and yelled, 'Do not lie to me. I can tell if you lie to me. How is Mrs. Eva?' Grand Papa Pete just said Mrs. Eva was her natural, normal self. He did not show fear at all. And he did not say one word about how crazy Mrs. Eva been acting, or how she shot her gun at Pastor Roberts. And Mrs. Jones did not know the difference. Ha! I could not believe it. A nice black cook traded some clothes and shoes for fish we caught."

"Here let me help you take your stuff off."

William took off the extra clothing and gave them to Daniel. Next, he showed Daniel the shoes.

"They got holes in them. But we can stuff the holes, and line the bottom of the shoes with rabbit fur. No more walking in the snow this winter without shoes. Yep! Last year, my feet cracked and bled until you could track me by my blood trail in the snow.

"And I saw a FREE BLACK MAN! He was dressed better than most white people here abouts and he had a beautiful chestnut stallion—fifteen hands high or better," William said. "What has been happening here?"

"Mrs. Eva, Mrs. Eva! Lord she has been on a war path. Be glad you were not here! Everyday someone got a flogging or beating. One day Overseer Graves asked her why she was whipping a woman from the tobacco barn. She said, 'Causes I can and I am making an example.' She nearly beat that woman to death over nothing.

"Mama came here and she was very upset and asked me to give you a hug. She left these little medicine bags for us to wear around our necks—one for you and one for me. If you get sick, she said, take some of the herbs and make a tea and drink it. And she left a message for Grand Papa Pete.

"A message for me?" said Pete as he entered the room. "Well, let us have supper and you can tell me about."

Pete looked around the room, confused by the disarray.

What happened here?" he asked.

"Overseer Graves and the new man Carter search the room. We do not know what they were looking for."

"No matter," said Pete. "Go and take care of those horses while I make us something to eat. Rub the horses down and remember to make sure they are cooled before you give them anything to drink."

The boys left the room and did as they were told. With tears in his eyes, Pete picked up his few belongings, put them back on the shelf, and started a fire in the small fireplace. He placed the fish, head and all, in a pot of water to make fish soup. He added a few grains of wild rice, wild peas, garlic, and wild onions he had gathered. Then, he rubbed the rabbit with sage and placed it on a spit to roast. He pulled out the last two biscuits the black cook had given him and waited for the boys to return.

"Mmm that smells good! This is a feast!" said Daniel.

"This is not a feast but it may be our last meal together," Pete said.

"What do you mean?" asked William.

"Enjoy the food. What did Mariah have to say?"

Daniel stopped eating and looked at Old Pete.

"She said a man stopped by the weaver's house and told her that Master Smith had lost a lot of money in New Orleans and there was going to be a slave auction!"

"We know about the slave auction," said William.

"Hush!" said Pete. "What else did she say?"

"She said we were not to come to the weaver's cabin anymore. She would try to meet us at the Hush Harbor meeting."

"Meet us at church," said William.

"Yes," said Daniel. "I love the Hush Harbor meetings. I love how we built a little church in the woods out of straw and twigs. I love the preaching, dancing, singing, and shouting when the holy spirit comes. And Sunday is the only day we have off and I love being with God on those days."

"Well," said William, "I wish God would help us a little more and get me away from Mrs. Eva."

They all laughed.

"Mama left these medicine bags to put around our necks. We are to make a tea from the stuff inside if we are sick. And she wanted you, Pete, to teach us about healing herbs."

"Did she say anything else?"

"Yes, she said that Master Smith was our pappy and we were not to tell anyone. I said if he was our pappy, surely, he would not sell us. She said he would! And if Mrs. Eva found out she would want us dead."

"Did the man tell her when Master Smith was coming home?"

"She did not say. She just said I should stick close to my brother and she hoped we would be sold together."

For a long while, the three souls were silent. The only sounds that could be heard were the crackling of the wood in the fireplace, rain as it fell on the roof, and in the distance the cry of a wolf or some other strange thing.

Finally, William asked, "What is a slave auction? I know we get sold, but how does it go?"

"Slave auction is a powerful, miserable, inhuman thing. There ain't nothing good about it. Families are torn apart never to be seen again. I lost my sweet Molly, Mariah's mother, in a slave auction. She was carrying my unborn child. That was a year after Mariah was born—1835. All I know is she was sold to somewhere in Tennessee."

"So... are you saying you are our granddaddy and Mariah is our mom for real?"

"Yes," said Old Pete.

"How do you know?" asked William.

"Well, I have the mark of a royal Nigerian family, and so did my mother. You, Mariah, and Daniel have that mark as well."

"What mark? I do not see any mark."

"Take your hand and feel the back of your head. Do you feel an area in the back of your head that feels like an egg, a hen egg?"

"Yes," said the boys.

"Let me see yours," they said to each other.

They examined each other's heads and Pete's head.

"Yes, we all have it. You are mine!" said Pete. "We are family! You are descendants of brave warriors and kings. And this mark has identified our line for generations. Now that is enough information for one night. Go to sleep. We will have a lot of work to do tomorrow."

CHAPTER EIGHT

Trapped!

Jenny, Miss Amy, Mrs. Eva, and Old Mama Sara had been packing things all evening. Anything of value in the house had been packed in crates. The first crate contained gold and silver dishes, fine china, and crystal. Crate two was filled with copper pots and kettles, and crate three abounded with fine rugs from China and tapestries from around the world. Most of these things were gifts from Mrs. Eva's father.

About 2:00 a.m. Mrs. Eva told Jenny to add wood to the fire in her room and after that she was free to go to bed. Jenny added the wood to the fire and left the flue to the fireplace open so she could hear Mrs. Eva if she called. She went downstairs to her small pallet next to the fireplace in the kitchen and laid down. She was almost asleep when she thought she heard a noise. She opened her eyes to see Old Sarah in the dining room with her ear to the stovepipe. Sarah raised her finger to Jenny, warning her to be quiet. Then she beckoned her to come closer. Through a vent in the stovepipe, they could hear Miss Amy and Mrs. Eva talking.

"I have sewn pockets in your skirts and jackets. Place the folding money in them and pin them pockets up tight. It is about ten thousand dollars. I will sew mother's diamond necklace and pearls into the hem of your waistcoat. In your purse, you will carry only a few gold coins—enough to buy tickets and food. The jewel case will contain some simple pieces of gold jewelry. Place the gold bangles on your arms and never remove your coat unless you are alone. Pack just a few things in the trunk and travel bag."

"What about all my other beautiful clothes?" asked Miss Amy.

"Amy, I have told you before! You cannot take them all. We have to be smart. Ed has a new woman in New Orleans and he will leave me as soon as this auction is over, taking all my money with him. We have to strike and get what we can before he gets here. It cannot look like you are trying to leave here never to return. We must take this opportunity and leave here with what we can.

"The telegram said Papa was sick and could not come but he was sending help. I do not know if that help will get here in time. I sold off some slaves to the Brown Plantation. Brown has paid me part of the money. He will pay the remainder when he picks the slaves up the day after Thanksgiving. Our cotton should be in by then.

"When the slaves find out about the slave auction, they will be upset and some may try to run," Mrs. Eva continued. "So, after Brown comes and gets the slaves he has purchased, I will separate the men from the women and children. I am going to lock the men up in the tobacco shed each night to guard them. The young women will be held in the cotton gin, and the children will be allowed to sleep in the slave hut with the older slaves. Separating the families will stop them from running off. Brown paid twenty thousand dollars for the slaves. I have given you the ten thousand dollars he paid me up front."

"Eva, you could just tell the slaves you are hiring them out to work until Christmas," Miss Amy said. "That is something they are used to doing and then they won't make a fuss."

"Maybe that can work," said Eva. "I do not want any problems until Papa's men get here. Mr. Jones wrote that Ed's flyer said the slave auction would occur on December fifteenth. Usually, slave dealers will try to see the slaves two to three days before an auction. That will make it about December twelfth. I do not know when Ed will be here. This is our only chance. If you miss this boat there will not be another before December fifteenth. So, stop your crying!

Stop that crying!"

Mrs. Eva shook her sister.

"Ed Smith has squandered my dowry of fifty slaves and forty thousand dollars in gold. He had the name and no money and we had money and no name so Papa made me marry him— and look what it has gotten me after six years. Not even a child!"

In a state of rage, Mrs. Eva said, "I am going to kill, beat, or sell every child Ed has sired, with a niggeress."

"Why? You can get top dollar for them, if they ain't all marked up," said Amy. "They are innocent anyway."

"I know but my pride will not allow it. It is bad enough that everyone knows he only married me for my money and that we aren't able to have kids. If they see his half breeds up for auction, they will whisper behind my back that I am a barren woman and Ed had to find his pleasures elsewhere. Oh, what a shame that would be!

"Now he has gone and lost all my money or given it to some whore in New Orleans—and we got to have a slave auction to boot. What a disgrace! I am not going have a group of high yellow niggers looking like Ed standing on the block adding insult to injury. If that woman in New Orleans came from a respectful family, Ed will have married her or promise to marry her and he will be plotting how to get rid of me. That is exactly what happened with his first wife, before we were married.

"So, I have made up my mind: I am going to strike first. I have made a list of every slave on this place. I know what they should fetch. The slaves, livestock, and furnishings, should bring two hundred and fifty thousand to five hundred thousand dollars or more. The problem is I do not know how much Ed owes."

"Are you going to give Old Sarah her freedom?" asked Amy.

"No, I can't," said Mrs. Eva. "I need every penny."

"But Sarah is old. You won't get much for her—two hundred dollars at the most. And you promised her. She has taken care of us as long as I can remember."

"I do not care! It does not mean a thang what you promise a nigger! I am selling her with the rest."

"Eva, how can you?"

"With a smile on my face and money to put in my pocket," she said.

When Old Sarah heard Eva's words she began to cry softly.

"Now hush up, Amy," said Eva. "Get to bed and I am going to called Old Pete at first light and you will be on your way to Camden by six a.m."

"Camden and not Cross Junction?" asked Amy.

"Camden!" I said, I do not want people to know you are gone, Amy."

"Carter will ride with you there and make sure you get on that boat. Then he must come back here to help me. You can take one little slave as your companion."

"I do not want a child. I want a big one!" said Amy. "And I want to say goodbye to my friends! I want—"

"What you want you ain't gonna get!" yelled Mrs. Eva. "You are going north and staying with Aunt Martha Sue in Philadelphia and you best try to find a rich husband while you are there—or you may find out what it really means to be called 'poor white trash.' Soon as I can I will join you. I will even send your things there if possible. Do not disappoint me. Now, who do you want to take?"

"Jenny!" said Amy.

"No, you can't have Jenny. I need her here."

"Carolyn, then!"

"Why do you want that mulatto, Carolyn?"

"Because she is the best seamstress for miles around and she makes lace almost as good as Mariah."

"Um," said Eva, "OK, you can take Carolyn. When I get there, she can make clothes for me and you both. I will send for her before daybreak and tell her to get ready."

"May I say goodbye to Old Mama Sarah and some of the children?"

"Hell no! These ain't your kin people. The less they know the better off we are. God put them slaves here in this world to make our life better! If they got to suffer then they got to suffer! Better them than us.

"Now Amy, when you are on that steamboat, stay in your cabin. Let Carolyn, get your meals. Keep this mourning veil on whenever you go out. Do not flirt with anyone. Do you remember the story you are to tell?"

"Yes, I do," said Amy.

"All right let me hear it."

"I am Amy Carter, and this is my brother Jed Carter. Our grandmother is very sick in Philly and I am on my way to help care for her with my slave Carolyn."

"Good, that is all you say! Let Carter buy the tickets for you and Carolyn. Tell Carolyn not to talk to anyone about you and this place. Treat her nice at least until you get to Philly. If she doesn't work out or gives you any kind of trouble you sell her quick! Quick, I say!"

"She is gonna want to take her little boy," said Amy.

"Tell her you and she will be back soon. She cannot take the little boy. He ain't worth nothing—fifty dollars at most. Have her leave the boy with Mama Sarah," Mrs. Eva said. "Here is a pistol. Always have it on your body. Use it if you have to, you hear! A war is coming! It will pit the south against the north. If the south loses, the life we know will be gone forever and these slaves may get their freedom. If they get freedom, some of them will not think kindly toward us."

Amy nodded her head in agreement.

"Eva, what are you gonna do with all those guns?"

"Worry yourself none about it."

"Are you sure Carter will come back to help you?"

"He will! Mr. Carter is trying to be my next husband. He will stay with you until you leave the shanty steamboat and get on the rail line bound for Philly. You will travel through Raleigh, North Carolina, to Richmond, Virginia, by boat. Then, by train, you go through Washington, DC, then Baltimore, Maryland, then Harrisburg, Pennsylvania, and from there to Philadelphia."

"Are you sure we can trust him?" ask Amy.

"We were friends before I married Ed Smith," said Eva. "Real good friends—if you know what I mean!"

"How are you going to pay him?"

"I am going to sell four or five slaves to the Barton Place before Carter returns and I will have the two thousand dollars I promised him and some extra. Trust no one, not even Carter! Understand, this is not a game, Amy, and the mistakes we make can cost us our lives. Go to bed now, I will wake you about four thirty."

Jenny and Old Sarah closed the stove vent and went back to the kitchen to lay down. Neither woman could sleep. The clock in the hall struck 3:00 a.m. In less than two hours their entire world would change forever.

Finally, Jenny laid down on her floor bed and muttered, "Trapped! Trapped! Trapped like a bear up a tree, in her sleep."

Sarah thought about how she had cared for Mrs. Eva and her family for more than fifty years, and how her dream of freedom would never come. This child she'd had to breastfeed said she was not worth $200. She turned her head toward heaven and cried.

Way off in the distance, Old Sarah thought she heard someone singing—or was that an animal howling? She closed her eyes and thought of so much pain! So much unbelievable PAIN! Even the wild things could feel the pain.

CHAPTER NINE

The Morning Crier

Old Grand Papa Pete had watched the Big House most of the night. He noticed that candles were lit all over the house until early morning. He could see Jenny and Sarah working, going from room to room. Mrs. Eva was up to something. He wondered why she needed the crates. Mrs. Eva was hot tempered and she was not going to take losing the plantation without a fight. He fell asleep and was woken by someone singing "Steal Away to Jesus" followed by an animal howl:

Steal away,
Steal away,
Steal away to Jesus.
Steal away,
Steal away home.
I ain't got long to stay here.

The song was a slave signal that the conductor of an underground railroad was near. But he did not know what the howl was about. He thought about running. He feared being sold downriver to Mississippi or to some cruel owner like Fred Brown. He felt despair like he had never felt before. Was he to lose the little family he had left? He was almost frozen with panic when the 4:30 a.m. whistle blew, signaling that it was time for slaves to get up and get ready for work by 5:00 a.m.

He wanted to be sure he was at the Big House before daylight as Mrs. Eva had ordered.

He looked at his grandsons and wondered if they would be allowed to come along. If Mrs. Eva would agree for the boys to come along on the trip, perhaps he and the boys could run to freedom. But he could not think of a single reason for her to do so. She had ordered everyone on the plantation to work from dawn to dust; and the boys were no exception. In fact, she had ordered everyone to the cotton field until the last cotton plant was picked and ready for market. Mrs. Eva had only made exceptions for kids under three, a few house slaves, and the men needed to tend the horses and cows.

He woke Willian and Daniel and said, "These are very dangerous times. Stay out of trouble if you can. William, keep out of Mrs. Eva's way. She will find a reason to whip someone each day. In the days to come, we may be sold and separated. But remember we are a family. Boys, I am going to nick the cartilage in your left ear so you may recognize each other if you are ever sold and separated one from another."

"I will always recognize my brother," said Daniel.

"This is just for insurance. Sometimes when people grow up their looks change."

Pete heated the end of a knife until it was red hot and he cut a small notch in Daniel's ear. He repeated the process and did the same to William. Then he pushed up his hair and marked his ear as well.

"I got to be at the Big House in a few minutes. Watch the wagon. If you see me with a hat on, it will mean that I am going on a trip and do not know when I am coming back. If there is no hat I expect to be back in a day or two. Boys, you are going to work with the horses today. Take them to the north field."

Anticipation filled the Big House. Jenny could hear Mrs. Eva walking back and forth.

Next, she heard the back stairs creak as she came into the kitchen.

"Morning, Mrs. Eva."

"You up early, Jenny."

"Yes ma'am, it is a wash day and I wanted to be sure I got enough hot water to wash the sheets and such."

"Go down to Carolyn's cabin and tell her to come here. I want her to go with Miss Amy on a small trip," said Mrs. Eva. "Have her take a bath before she comes and put on her best dress. Tell her Grandma Sarah will take care of her son while she is gone."

"Yes'm," said Jenny.

"On your way back tell Old Pete to hitch a team of horses that can carry a heavy load. I will be sending him on an errand."

"Yes ma'am."

"And tell him do not come before six a.m."

"Yes'm," said Jenny.

Jenny left the kitchen and headed toward the slave quarters.

"Sarah, make Miss Amy her favorite breakfast today," said Mrs. Eva. "She is going on a little trip. Make some sandwiches for her to eat later. Put some cookies and cakes in the picnic basket." Mrs. Eva went into the pantry and began to fill the basket with canned meats, dried fruits, crackers, and other candy sweets.

"Yes'm, I be glad to do it," said Sarah. "You know I love you children like you were my own. And I hope to see the day Miss Amy is twenty-one."

"Why?" asked Eva.

"Why Mrs. Eva, you joke," said Sarah. "That is the day you promised to give me my freedom. It's been almost fifteen years since you made that promise. You wouldn't break it, now, would you?"

"No Sarah," said Eva comely. "One day you will be free."

Sarah looked at Mrs. Eva, remembering, what she had heard Eva say the night before, and realized that she could and would lie with ease. At that moment, she knew Mrs. Eva would never give her freedom papers.

"Go and sit at the dining room table. I will bring your breakfast just the way you like it." When Eva left the room, Old Sarah dipped up some grits, spat in them, and mixed the spit and grits on Mrs. Eva's plate. She then mixed cotton root in her tea to prevent pregnancy. Mrs. Eva had sold Sarah's children and she was determined to keep her from having any! This tonic of the cotton root would stop if Mrs. Eva would give her freedom, and Eva would have the children she wanted.

She put a smile on her face and walked in the dining room and said, "Here is your breakfast, Mrs. Eva, just like you deserve!" She then turned and walk back into the kitchen.

At 5:00 a.m. a warning bell rang. It meant that slaves should be ready to go to work. They had just enough time to get their tools and get a handful of corn pone. They were expected to assemble in front of the barn before going to work. There was a line of 150 slaves going to the cotton fields to gather the last of the cotton. Also, about twenty-five souls were sent to the tobacco shed to work. Three women were sent to a spinning room to make fabric and lace. Of the remainder, ten men cut timber and twelve or more boys and men were working with the horses and painting the barn and mending fences.

Overseer Graves pulled out twelve men ages twenty to forty-five and told them to wait in the field in front of the barn while he sent the others to work. It was only fifteen minutes after 5:00 a.m. and everyone was in their place working, all before sunrise.

Pete fed the horses and went to the Big House. He wondered what Mrs. Eva wanted with the ten to twelve men sitting on the ground.

"Frank, do you know why those boys are there?"

"Yes," said Frank. "Overseer Graves stopped by my cabin this morning and said I was to get chains ready to lash those boys to a wagon. They are going to work for hire down on the Brown Plantation. I feel sorry for those boys. Master Brown is a cruel bastard that takes pleasure in hurting and maiming slaves. I have heard it rumored that he likes sleeping with boys—the younger the better. Tell William and

Daniel to stay away from the barn if they can while he is here. He takes pride in 'breaking in a boy or man.'"

"What do you mean?"

"Well, he chooses one, bends them over, ties them down, and then rapes that man or boy. He enjoys it. Then that man or boy has to have sex with him on demand. All the other slaves are forced to watch. He is a 'homo.' That's why most slave owners do not lend their male slaves out to work on the Brown Plantation, but they will sell slaves to him. He is as low as they come."

"Is he here yet?" asked Pete.

"Not that I can see. Overseer Graves said he would be here directly."

Old Grand Papa Pete and Frank were going to the Big House when Jenny waved for them to stop.

"Hey Jenny, did you know Brown is coming here today?"

"No!" she said. "That is bad! Really bad! I got to run and fetch Carolyn. She will be going with you today."

"Jenny, could you tell Mrs. Eva that the boys have a fever or send them away from the barn while Brown is here."

"I can't. Mrs. Eva is going to be mad when she finds out Brown is on his way. She was not expecting him until after Thanksgiving. If he sees your boys, he will try to have his way with them."

"Overseer Graves said Master Brown was fetching the boys to hire out on his plantation."

"I will do what I can," said Jenny, "but Mrs. Eva done sold them boys to Brown and she don't want no one to know. Most of them will be hurt bad or raped in no time. On the Brown place, most slaves only last a few years. Brown is sick in the head. Mrs. Eva sent me down here to tell you not to come before six a.m. and to bring a team of horses to the kitchen that can pull a heavy load. And she wants a covered wagon with an extra seat. Go back to the barn and I will call you when she is ready!"

Old Grand Papa Pete and Frank turned around toward the barn. When Frank saw Overseer Graves he said, "Overseer Graves, it would be a blessing if William and Daniel could go and get some hog and cow medicine. We need to worm the pigs before hog-killing time."

Graves paused for a minute and said, "That will be fine. Tell them boys they must be back by nightfall and keep clear of strangers on this place today. Tom Brown will be here today with all of his strange appetites. I like those boys," Graves said, "and I want them to stay boys as long as they can."

Pete, Graves, and Frank locked eyes with one another and without saying a word knew that Graves was trying to keep the boys from getting raped. Pete ran ahead to send the boys on their way.

When Jenny came to the slave's quarter, she had to pass Nana Dawson's cabin. She hated how that old woman poured the food in a trough outside her cabin and had the babies eat with their hands like she was feeding piglets. She had nothing to say to her. She despised her and her hateful ways. She quickly passed by and went to the weaver's cabin.

The women were already working. She said, "Carolyn, Mrs. Eva wants you to work at the Big House. She says you are to take a bath and bring clothes for the week or more. Mama Sarah will be taking care of your boy, Emmanuel, while you work. Hurry, you need to be in the kitchen before six o'clock." Jenny wanted to tell Carolyn more but she couldn't get her alone. So, as she was leaving, she said, "Hurry, Carolyn, and give your son a big kiss and hug from me."

When Jenny returned to the Big House no one was in the kitchen. Sarah was in the dining room clearing away the breakfast dishes. She beckoned Jenny to listen at the stovepipe.

"You listen and I will keep watch," she said.

Slowly Jenny opened the pipe and listened.

Mrs. Eva said, "Brown sent word he is coming here today between five thirty and six and not to send the slaves I have sold him to the field. I wonder why he decided to come today. He is not getting the slaves without paying me."

"How many slaves did you sell him?" asked Miss Amy.

"Twelve young bachelors at twelve hundred to sixteen hundred apiece will fetch anywhere from fourteen thousand and four hundred dollars to nineteen thousand and two hundred dollars."

"Won't the slaves put up a fuss?"

"I do not think so. I told them and Overseer Graves they are going on a work detail and will be back by Christmas."

"Now that is smart," said Amy.

"Amy, put on a house dress, like you are just coming down for breakfast. Do not say anything about leaving. I want him to see you. If he tries to talk to you tell him you have a sore throat or something and you need to go back upstairs and go to bed."

After hearing this, Jenny closed the stovepipe and went back to the kitchen with Sarah. At five thirty on the dot Master Brown knocked on the door. Jenny bowed and cursed under her breath as she opened the door.

He said, "Tell Eva that Brown is here!"

Jenny invited him into the parlor, closed the door, and went to get Mrs. Eva.

Eva came down the stairs, sporting a rifle. She exchanged pleasantries with Brown and offered him coffee.

"No thanks," he said. "I want this deal over and done with. What are you doing with that rifle?"

"I am going hunting this morning."

"Good!" he said, "back to our deal. I plan to leave here within an hour."

"Fine with me," said Eva. "Just show me your coins. I have twelve slaves for you in prime condition."

"Have them brought round," said Brown.

"All right," said Eva. She went to the door and yelled, "Graves, have those boys run over here."

"Now Mrs. Eva, I usually get to sample the goods before I buy."

She laughed and said, "There will be none of your kind of sampling here."

"Why Mrs. Eva, what have folks been saying about me?"

"Only the truth! The God-honest truth, Brown."

At that moment, Amy passed the parlor door.

"Why Miss Amy, come and sit for a while," said Brown.

"I can't, sir. I am feeling might poorly. I am having one of my headaches. I need to lay down. Next, time for sure." She called to the kitchen, "Jenny, bring my tea and medicine upstairs."

When Brown turned around, Eva had her rifle raised and pointed at his head.

"Back to business," she said. "Money or else get off my place."

"I brought you money, Eva. No cause for that! How about sixteen thousand for the lot? I have already given you ten thousand, and I will give you six thousand today, in gold, as you asked."

"Sixteen thousand dollars is a nice sum, but those slaves are worth more."

"True!" said Brown. "Truth be told, Mrs. Eva, you are at a small disadvantage with a slave auction coming soon here about."

"All right," said Eva. "I believe in a fair deal—more than my daddy and brothers. They will be here tomorrow or the next day. They are more particular with whom they deal with than me. What about eighteen thousand dollars? You will just have to give me eight thousand more. That way we have split the difference down the middle."

"Deal! he said. I will need a bill of sale."

"No problem. My daddy gave me fifty slaves when I married Ed. By law those slaves are mine. Your bill of sale will be free and clear."

"All right," he said and counted out the gold coins and placed them on the table. "Don't you want to count it?"

"No need! I'll take your word for it. And if I am short my papa and my brothers and their Smith and Wessons will take it out of your hide," she said with a smile.

Brown picked up his hat and went out of the door. He had the men chained to the wagon, said goodbye to Eva, and drove down the lane with Cherokee Big Knife and his dogs following close behind. He did not want any problems with Eva's family. They were as crazy as they come and dead shots to boot. He had got what he came for, the slaves, but more importantly the knowledge that she expected her brothers to be at her plantation in one or two days. He would warn Ed Smith, if he could, and make even more money.

Mrs. Eva watched with her rifle in hand, until Brown, the slaves, and Cherokee Big Knife had cleared the lane and were on the main road. She watched to see if he was headed to town or if he was going in the other direction. He was heading away from town, which meant he did not want anyone to ask about the slaves.

Mrs. Eva was visibly shaken. She walked from the veranda, poured herself a large bourbon, drank it, and called Amy.

"Amy, get dressed and be ready to go in a few minutes," she said.

Next, she called Jenny and said, "Go to the barn and tell Pete and Frank to come and load the wagon. Remind Pete he will need horses that can pull a heavy load over rough ground. Tell him to load the wagon from the kitchen."

"Is Carolyn here?"

"Yes ma'am. She is in the kitchen."

Jenny ran to the barn to get Pete and Frank. Soon Pete drove up to the Big House with a team of four hardy Indian ponies and a covered wagon with two rows of seats. Frank and Pete loaded the wagon and covered the back and front openings with tarps, ensuring that the tarp covered the second seat.

"Old Pete, this is Flint Carter. He is a friend of mine and he will be traveling with you to Camden and so will Miss Amy and Carolyn."

"Ma'am, it is cold this time of year in the mountains. We may get snow. They need to dress warmly."

"I want you and Frank to go upstairs and get Amy's trunk and bag."

"Yes, Mrs. Eva."

In a few minutes, Frank and Pete came down the stairs with the trunk. Miss Amy got on the second seat with a basket. She wore a dust cover to keep her boat travel clothes clean. Old Sarah covered her with quilts to keep warm.

As Carolyn was about to get in the back of the wagon Jenny said, "Carolyn, please come and get these meds for Miss Amy, just in case she gets sick." Carolyn ran back to the kitchen to get the meds.

"Wait," said Jenny. "I got something to tell you and don't you holler nor cry. Miss Amy is going north and so is you! If she gets sick, never throw out her traveling clothes. Money and jewels are in them clothes and those crates contain valuable items. You are an octoroon and can pass for any white woman. I will take care of your son. If you get a chance for freedom, take it. Go now!"

Carolyn looked stunned. Hopelessness filled her heart. She wanted to scream.

"If you cry or act differently Mrs. Eva will know I told you and she will kill me and your little boy before the noonday sun just to keep folks from knowing Miss Amy is going somewhere." Then Jenny said, "I think that is everything Carolyn—see you soon."

"OK," said Carolyn.

"Mighty fine horse you riding," Mrs. Eva said to Flint Carter. "Looks like an Arabian stallion. I have never seen a horse like him in these parts."

"He is a beauty," said Flint Carter. "Picked him up for a song and a steal from a man down on his luck."

Pete looked at the horse and knew it was the freed black man's horse and said not a word.

Mr. Carter said, "I think Frank should come just in case we have trouble. We may need his help if we have trouble with the wagon and this heavy load."

"All right," said Eva. "I can spare him for a day or so."

Frank said, "May I run and get my old coat to keep warm?"

"Yes," said Carter.

He ran to the barn, got his coat, his med bag, two gold coins he had found in the streets of New Orleans when he was a boy, and a small knife he kept hidden in the barn.

Carolyn got in the bed of the wagon and sat down on the floor. Pete closed the back opening with a tarp and tied it securely. Mrs. Eva kissed Miss Amy and said, "Pete, I do not want anyone to see Miss Amy. Cover this front opening good!" Pete pulled the wagon cover over the second seat and added an additional tarp to cover the opening.

"Are you all right in there, Miss Amy?" he asked.

"Yes, I am fine."

"After we hit the Camden road you will be able to come out. There are not many people in the mountains."

Pete put on his hat as a signal to the boys that he was going on a long trip. He hoped that they would see it. Frank took a seat on the wagon next to Pete.

Mrs. Eva said, "Pete, drive the back way out of the plantation, over the south road to Clark Junction then take the Camden road and go over the mountain."

"Yes'm," he said.

Pete walked around the wagon once more, checking the harness, bridle, bit, clocker, reins, breaching, and back saddle for each horse. Next, he checked the trace. All was in order.

"Ready to go," he said as he climbed on the wagon driver's seat.

"Well Eva, we must get going," said Flint Carter. "I will be back in a few days."

Pete started the team of horses down the road and away they went. Carolyn laid in the back of the wagon and tears ran down her face. Miss Amy laid her head on the basket and started to fall asleep. Flint Carter followed behind with his rifle at the ready and his two hounds running alongside.

CHAPTER TEN

Riding with the Devil

Pete did not trust this Mr. Carter. It was clear he was riding the freed black man's horse. What he did not know was whether Carter stole the horse or bought it from someone, but he knew whoever took the horse had left the black man for dead.

The first part of their trip was very uneventful. They traveled the south road to Clark Junction without seeing a soul. A few people were at the store at Clark Junction—mostly travelers going south. They watered the horses and kept moving. Finally, they took the Camden road leading to the mountains.

The North Carolina mountains were a joy to behold. They looked like a painting. Great oaks and pine trees gave way to open grassy areas called balds. Rhododendron plants were everywhere. There were numerous clean, clear mountain streams. They saw plenty of deer, elk, rabbits, squirrels, geese, and wild turkeys. When they came to the Roam Overlook, they marveled at the waterfall in one direction and snow-covered mountain peaks in the other. No one uttered a word.

Finally, Frank said, "I have never seen anything so pretty as these North Carolina mountains. If I was freed, I'd live in these mountains."

Old Pete chuckled and said, "If I was free, I would get the hell out of North Carolina."

Both men laughed.

Midafternoon they stopped to water the horses and get a quick bite to eat. Miss Amy complained about her headache. Carolyn made her a place to lay down in the back of the wagon and gave her some of the meds Doctor Baker had prescribed. After an hour of rest, Mr. Carter said, "We need to keep moving. We will not make it to Camden before dark. So, we will have to spend the night in the mountains. I am hoping we will reach the hunter's cabin and will be able to stay there tonight."

Although the mountain had peaks, what they referred to as "crossing the mountain" was not a single peak but a twenty-mile-long ridge that wrapped around the mountain straddling North Carolina and parts of Virginia.

"In case, it gets too late and we can't make it to the cabin, Pete, keep an eye out for a place for us to stay tonight. I want to keep traveling as long as we can."

Pete nodded.

"I am not sure how close we are. I am going to scout ahead," said Carter.

Near nightfall, Carter returned and said, "There is a little bald grassy area on the left in a mile or two. Pull in and follow me. We will camp here tonight. It will have to be a cold camp. I do not want to attract unwelcome attention. Feed and water the horses, boys, then I will have to chain you to that tree yonder. My hunting dogs will stand watch. Mind you, boys, if I say the words these dogs will tear the throat out of any man."

Carolyn gave everyone a sandwich and they all went to sleep except Old Pete. He kept watch and wondered if he could run for freedom.

The next morning, they continued to Camden. By noon they were out of the mountains and headed down into the valley. They were only about two hours from Camden when a powerful rainstorm hit. It was a monster of a storm, with large balls of hail. They took cover in an old cabin at the end of a clearing.

Pete drove the horses around the back of the cabin and Miss Amy and Carolyn ran inside. Old Pete found shelter for the horses in a nearby lean-to. Carter did a quick check around the cabin. Then he stood guard at the door. Frank brought in some wood to make a fire. He was glad he had stored some wood in the wagon. Carolyn cooked some corn cakes on the fire and opened two cans of beans. Peter and Frank dried the horses.

After they had eaten, Carter said, "It ain't fitting for you nigger boys to be in the same cabin as a white woman. As soon as this storm lets up, I am going to tie you to the wagon."

"They are going to just about freeze if you do," said Miss Amy.

"Never you mind," said Carter, "that is what is going to happen."

When there was a small break in the weather, Carter marched Frank and Old Papa Pete outside and tied them to the wagon. The men scampered under the wagon and huddled together to get out of the freezing rain. Flint Carter went back into the cabin and stood guard at the door.

"I ain't never seen a storm like this in all my years," he said. "There are signs that someone used this cabin from time to time. I cannot tell if they are white or Indian. We need to keep watch."

Carolyn went to check on Amy, who was lying on the floor in front of the fire.

"Is she asleep?" asked Carter.

"Yes sir. I think she has a fever."

"Do we have anything to give her for a fever?" he asked.

"No sir. She took all the medicine the doctor gave her. Poor thang," she said, "the doctor's medicine does not do any good. Old Pete is a slave doctor—maybe he can help," said Carolyn.

Carter did not want to ask Pete for help. He did not know what kind of foolish slave meds Old Pete had, and it probably would not work anyway. So, he told Carolyn to keep cold compresses on Amy's head and she would be better in the morning.

"Yes sir," she said.

As the storm raged, they could hear loud claps of thunder and saw lighting flashing through the sky. Midafternoon passed into night. The storm did not let up. The dogs whined and whimpered at the door. Finally, around 11:00 p.m. Carter let his dogs into the cabin. Miss Amy woke at about 1:00 a.m. She was burning up with a fever and complaining about her head hurting. She went in and out of consciousness.

Around 3:00 a.m. she yelled, "Help me Old Pete! Give me some of your medicine," and passed out.

"We need to get her some help or she is a goner for sure," said Carolyn. "Sir, can we see if Old Pete can help. Mrs. Eva will be powerful mad if anything happens to her sister."

Flint Carter did not respond. He knelt over Miss Amy and checked her forehead for fever; she was very hot to the touch. After a few minutes, he put on his slicker and went to get Old Pete.

Pete looked at Miss Amy and asked that they move her closer to the fireplace.

"I am going to make her some tea. We need to keep her sitting up. It will help her breathe."

Pete made Amy a tea using sage and pennyroyal.

"Drink it all. You will feel better tomorrow."

She drank the tea and laid down.

"What is that tea supposed to do?" asked Carter.

"Well, the sage will help with a sore throat and pennyroyal fights colds, reduces fevers, and sometimes helps headaches," answered Pete.

"You better be right. If not, I am going to take the whip to you for sure."

The storm stopped shortly before daybreak. It had become extremely cold. Carolyn made a small breakfast. Pete stood watch as Mr. Carter slept. Miss Amy woke and said, "I am hungry, but I feel so much better.

"Looks like your fever broke," said Carolyn.

"Pete, may I have more of that tea?"

"Yes ma'am."

Amy walked over and looked out the window. "Mr. Carter, do you think the storm is over?" she exclaimed.

"Hope so, Miss Amy. Pete, go untie Frank and help him feed and water the horses." Frank's clothes were frozen to him. Ice was in his eyebrows and beard. Pete built a small fire to help remove the frozen clothes. Frank put on his other shirt that was in the wagon and covered himself with a horse blanket. They fed and watered the horses and stayed by the fire to keep warm and to try and dry their clothes.

Frank muttered, "He treated his dogs better than us. The dogs were able to get shelter from the rain in the cabin. Look what happened to us."

"Hush!" said Old Pete. "It ain't gonna do no good to complain."

Flint Carter opened the door and yelled, "Have those horses and wagon ready to go in an hour."

"Yes sir," said Pete.

Frank rolled his eyes and said nothing.

CHAPTER ELEVEN

Camden

Within the hour, Frank and Pete pulled the wagon up to the door and waited to continue the journey to Camden. The road was littered with tree limbs and bushes. Frank went in front of the wagon, clearing the trail so the wagon could move down the road safely, and Flint Carter scouted ahead. The large hounds trotted behind the wagon.

Finally, they reached a bluff overlooking Camden. They were not expecting much, just a small store, cotton gin, and the beginnings of a lumber mill with a stable and bunkhouse for the lumberjacks—about ten to twelve people.

"Looks like the storm hit the settlement pretty hard," said Pete. "It tore off the roof."

"Something is on fire. Wait here," said Mr. Carter. "I am going to ride ahead and see what is wrong. It could have been the storm or maybe they had other kinds of trouble. Pete, pull the wagon up in those trees. Miss Amy and Carolyn do not come out of the wagon until I tell you." And he galloped down the road.

Later, they heard Carter yelling, "Come quick—come a running—COME A RUNNING!"

Nothing could prepare them for the devastation. Men and women lay dead in the street. Large trees had their bark peeled off from top to bottom, like someone was peeling an apple. Tall pine trees were snapped in half. The lumber mill had exploded into large toothpick-sized pieces. The cotton gin was on fire. The general store had been torn to bits. Clothing and house goods were everywhere. The roof was torn off the bunkhouse. Two people were hanging dead from the trees. Several dead horses lay in the street. The road leading to the river had been washed away.

"What happened?" asked Carter.

"Tornado! Tornado! All is lost. The tornado even picked up the steamboat and smashed it into the rocks," one of the survivors said.

"Help us dig some graves and leave this place—you can't stay in these mountains without food and shelter. We need to burn the dead animals so we won't be plagued by mountain lions and bears looking for food tonight," said the scared little man.

Flint Carter was at a loss. He had seen dead people before, but never had he seen the dead with so many injuries. Of the fifteen people who lived in Camden, ten were dead: eight men and two women. The living included Bret Garrison, his wife Sue Ellen, and their son, Arthur, and Mrs. Harry Burns and her three-month-old daughter Jasmine. The survivors were wet, cold, and in shock.

"Pete, Frank, Carolyn, and Miss Amy, come over and help. Pete, take everyone to the bunkhouse. It doesn't have a roof but it does have four walls. Frank, build a good fire. I am going to see if I can find enough horses so we can ride out of here. While I am gone, Pete and Frank, help Mr. Garrison dig a grave—just one large grave. Mrs. Garrison, see if you can find something to cook. And Carolyn, prepare the dead for burial as best you can. Look in their pockets and bring their valuables to me!"

Mrs. Garrison started supper from the supplies found in the bunkhouse. Miss Amy and Mrs. Burns looked after the children. Carolyn took a basin of water and soap and went to each dead body and washed its face. She hated robbing the dead, but she had no choice.

Thus, she looked for anything of value to bring back to Flint Carter. A watch, a ring, some paper money— there was so little.

When she was looking through the pockets of the man, they called Burns, the owner of the cotton gin, she found his freedom papers. Freedom papers. Then she realized Harry Burns with the freckles was a Negro, and passing for white—perhaps he was an octoroon like her, which was seven-eights white and one-eighth black, or quadroon, which meant he was three-quarters white and one-quarter black. Carolyn finished her job, but she realized that Negroes could really pass for white. They could have freedom, power, and money just like the whites, she thought. She brought all items she found back for Flint Carter except the freedom papers. She pinned those papers to her slip.

Mrs. Burns said, "Thank you. Would you please give me my husband's things?"

" Yes'm, here is the watch I found and some paper money."

"Thank you! Did you find anything else?"

"Not of value ma'am, just some paper I burned in a fire before it caused good folks some harm."

She watched to see if she would get a reaction for Mrs. Burns. The woman looked at her but said nothing.

Late in the evening, Flint Carter retuned with four horses. The bodies were buried.

Mrs. Burns said, "Pete and Frank, if you help me gather what few belongings I have left and put them in my wagon you may have a set of clothing or anything else you want from the store. I can't stay here. In the morning, I am going to Beck Spur and catching the train north to return to my family. Ain't nothing for me here. Frank, you look like the size of my husband. He was a big man too. I would be proud if you'd find something of his to wear."

"Train, did you say?" asked Flint Carter. "I did not know a train was coming up to the mountain."

"Yes, it has been in Beck Spur for almost three months. It is a lumber train and you can get a passenger train down the line at Winder and from there the train will take you across Virginia to Philly and then to New York City."

"Miss Amy was trying to catch the boat to go to Philly to care for her sick grandmother. I thought we would not be able to get there, but now she can ride the train. What a blessing," he said. "How far is it?"

"About ten to fifteen miles."

"Do you think we could get there before noon?"

"Maybe said," Mrs. Burns. "Last time I went with my husband it took about four hours or so."

"Well, then let us all turn in for a good night's rest. We deserve it. Be ready to leave by seven a.m. tomorrow."

CHAPTER TWELVE

Beck Spur

The next morning, Mrs. Burns got up at daybreak, went to her store, and looked through its burned-out shell. She found some canned milk and food in the storeroom. She opened the door to the underground root cellar. There, she found work clothing, a few dresses she had ordered, a large quilt and several blankets, and various tools. But most important of all she found the cash box hidden below some loose bricks in the cellar. It contained five thousand dollars in gold—enough money to give her and the baby a new start. She placed the gold, a blanket, milk, dresses, and two pair of women's boots in a sack.

When she returned to the bunkhouse, she said, "There, are a few good things in the cellar. Frank, would you and Pete go and place them in my wagon. There are some flannel shirts—keep one for each of you."

"Where is everyone?" she asked, looking around.

"Miss Amy and Mrs. Garrison went to the outhouse and Mr. Carter and Mr. Garrison decide to look and see if there was anything of value at the sawmill or cotton gin," Carolyn said.

"Carolyn, here are some boots; you may have them," Mrs. Burns said. "I noticed your shoes were worn out. My papa used to say a man judges a woman by her shoes. Shoes, clothing, and one's hair separate a wealthy woman from a poor one—even a slave from its master. Why, I hear tell that some slave girls with fair skin and 'good' hair pass for white all the time—and in places like New York or Canada, black men and women are free no matter the color of their skin. Maybe you can go to Canada one day."

Carolyn did not say a word. She acted as if she did not understand. This kind of talk could get her killed. Who was this woman? Finally, Carolyn said, "I got to hurry, Mrs. Burns. Miss Amy will be here any minute and I must have everything ready for her.

"Well, since we are to be ready by seven a.m. I am going to check on the baby and change my clothes," said Mrs. Burns.

Mrs. Burns picked up her baby, looked around, went to the back room. She closed the door and placed the gold in the baby's blanket and draped a quilt over the baby to keep her warm. She changed her dress, put on the new boots, and combed her hair. Next, she joined the others for breakfast.

The others soon returned.

"I saw you look through the ashes of your store," said Amy.

"Yes, I was saying goodbye to my dreams and I was hoping to find a picture or some token of my husband, but there was nothing—just a bit of food, clothing, and such."

"Well! Well!" said Bret Garrison, "We have our memories. We must be on our way if we are going to get to Beck Spur before the train leaves today. It will be the last one before spring. Personally, I never want to see these mountains again. Mr. Carter, if your group is coming, let us get started."

"Mr. Carter, sir, do you think I could rent one of your men slaves to drive my wagon to Beck Spur?"

"Why yes ma'am, you can."

"Would ten dollars be a fair price?" she asked.

"Why of course, ma'am, that will be fine. I will have to pay you when I get to Beck Spur—we all got money coming."

"Yes, indeed," said Garrison, "three months' pay. Plus, money from the timber that they will be picking up today at two o'clock this afternoon."

"Ma'am I covered your wagon with a tarp I found in the bunkhouse. It will help you and the baby stay warm."

"Thank you, Pete."

"Frank will have to drive your wagon. He cannot handle a four-horse team."

Mrs. Harrison got in the wagon and place a pistol in her waistcoat and rifle across her lap.

"Do you need all that firepower, miss?" asked Flint Carter.

"Yes, I do, sir. I plan to protect me and mine."

"Mrs. Burns ain't no stranger to guns, Mr. Carter," said Garrison. "That lady is a dead shot with pistol or rifle. If we have trouble, you will be mighty glad she came along."

"Let's go!" she said and with that, the three wagons headed toward Beck Spur. Garrison's wagon led the way, followed by the wagon with Old Pete, Miss Amy, and Carolyn. The last wagon contained Frank and Mrs. Burns and the baby. Flint Carter and his dogs went ahead to scout the way.

CHAPTER THIRTEEN

Stolen

As they started down the logging road the sky became dark, as if it was going to rain, and the dark color of the sky made everyone a little nervous. Mrs. Burns decided to climb in the back of the wagon to check on her baby. After a while, she said, "That is a very fine horse Mr. Carter is riding. Do you have many horses like that on his plantation?"

"Ma'am, I don't know. I don't think he owns a plantation. Pete and me belong to Miss Amy's sister, Mrs. Eva, and her husband Master Ed. Smith. But no, we don't have horses like that on Round Pond Plantation. That horse is the first Arabian stallion we have ever seen around Cross Junction. It sho' is mighty fine!

"Frank, has Mr. Carter lived in Cross Junction for a long time?"

"No ma'am, he just came to the plantation a few days ago. He is a friend of Miss Amy's sister, Mrs. Eva Smith. Mrs. Eva hired him to take Miss Amy to Camden to get on the riverboat, and here we is."

"I see," she said. "Can't you get on the riverboat at Cross Junction?"

"Yes ma'am, you can, but Mrs. Eva was in a hurry for Miss Amy to catch the boat north."

"Thank you," she said.

"Ma'am, thank you for the clothes and boots. This flannel shirt is mighty fine! Mighty fine!"

"My pleasure," she said. "Frank, do they have freed black men in your area?"

"Ma'am, one or two old men were given their freedom some time back, but they dead now."

They drove down the road in silence. Frank wondered what it would be like to be free to go where you wanted, do what you will, and maybe have a wife and family—and maybe own several warm flannel shirts.

Mrs. Burns knew that the horse Flint Carter was riding belonged to her half-brother. Their father had given it to him when he had given him his freedom papers. Only death could have parted him from the horse. And she knew Flint Carter was a thief and maybe a murderer. She decided to watch, keep her guns close, and pray they reach Beck Spur quickly. She wondered if Carolyn had found the freedom papers on her husband. They had lived as a white couple in Camden. Most people assumed he was white because of his freckles. He loved the North Carolina mountains and he wanted to stay there. But since he was dead, she had made up her mind to get on that train and flee to Canada—flee to freedom no matter the cost.

A couple of hours later she heard a strange yell.

"What is that Frank? Trouble?"

"No ma'am, that is old Pete. He always makes that yell when arrives where he is a-going." She peeked out the wagon and she could see Beck Spur and the train waiting at the station. Men were loading the timber on the train, and the few townspeople were going about their daily chores.

"Stop at the lumberyard," she said. "I got some business to do there and then we will go to the train."

Frank did as he was told. She got out of the wagon, took the baby with her, and went into the office of the lumber mill.

"Hello, Mrs. Burns," said Mr. Walter, the manager of the lumber mill. "I did not expect you here until next week."

"A tornado hit Camden and all is lost, even my husband. I need to pick up the money we left here for safekeeping and my share of the lumber that will be shipped today."

"Sorry about your loss," he said. "Ma'am, you know you can't stay in those mountains alone. What are you planning on doing?"

"I know. I am going to catch the train back to Virginia and go and live with my folks."

He walked to the safe and opened it.

"Here is the package your husband left for safekeeping, and your share of the lumber we are shipping today comes to two thousand, five hundred dollars."

"Is that all? We were expecting much more."

"Well, I'll throw in another thousand because the company will not have to pay the dead."

"Thanks," she said, and left the store.

When she got to the train, the others were waiting for her. Amy and Carolyn had their tickets and had taken their seats on the train. She bought a ticket for herself and the baby. She turned to Flint Carter and said, "Would you sell one of your slaves? I am gonna need someone to help me get to my father's plantation."

He thought for a minute and said, "These slaves are worth a lot of money: two thousand, five hundred dollars for Pete and sixteen hundred for Frank."

"Well, that is more than I can afford," she said, and turned toward the train.

"What can you afford?"

"Eight hundred is as high as I can go, plus the wagon, horses, and food supplies—you would get an extra five hundred to six hundred more."

Carter thought for a minute. Then he said, "It's a deal."

She peeled off eight hundred dollars and gave it to him.

"Frank," he yelled. "You now belong to Mrs. Burns. Get on that train."

"But sir I—"

"Ma'am, here are some shackles for him to wear. Put this key around your neck and let the train men handle the rest."

She climbed on the train and gave the porter fare for Frank.

Just like that Frank had been sold by a man who didn't even own him. He would never see his wife and children again, nor his beloved mother. He had been set adrift. He would be forever lost to his family!

Frank was shackled and placed on the train in the baggage car. He looked at Pete with tears in his eyes and said, "Tell 'em, I be sold . . . going somewhere in Virginia, I think. Lord! Lord!"

Before he knew it, Old Pete said, "Mr. Carter, you can't sell Mrs. Eva's slave!"

As quick as a flash, Flint Carter took his cane and hit Old Pete across the face, breaking his jaw. Pete fell to the ground and Flint Carter stomped him in the chest and kicked him in the ribs.

"Can't no nigger tell me what to do!" he said. He spat on him for good measure.

Mr. Mills, the storekeeper, said, "I will have Indian Joe drive Mrs. Burns's wagon to the store. Then he can come back and bring Mrs. Eva's wagon as well. Don't look like your slave able to do it."

Old Pete got on his knees and tried to stand. He mumbled, "May I say goodbye to Frank, sir? We have been friends for more than thirty years."

"No need," he said, "y'all don't feel the way white folks do. He'll be fine."

"What you gonna say to Mrs. Eva bout selling her—"

He stopped midsentence when he saw Flint Carter's eyes. "Pete, you need to worry about your own life—what little you got left."

Blood filled Pete's mouth and nose and he realized he could not move his jaw when he tried to spit out the blood and mucus.

Storekeeper Mills said, "Make up your mind, Carter. Kill that nigger or let him live. I thought we were going to celebrate. The ladies at the Circle C Saloon are waiting."

Carter looked at Mills and said, "Let's go—don't want to keep the ladies waiting. I think five hundred dollars should be a fair price for Mrs. Burns' team and wagon, what do you say?"

"Well . . . Ok," said Mills, "It is a deal. Then the drinks are on me. Indian Joe and Ray Ren, take that slave over to my store and chain him to a post in the barn. Cool down and feed Mr. Carters horses."

Without another word, the men grabbed Pete, carried him away, and chained him to a post in the barn.

"How long do you plan on staying in Beck Spur?" Mr. Mills asked Mr. Carter.

"Well, I will be staying in town tonight . . . maybe tomorrow. I got some celebrating to do," said Carter. "Have your man give my slave a bit of food and water."

"No sooner said than done," said Mills. As the two men were walking away, Carter yelled, "My stallion is sort of funny! Make sure Pete brushes and cares for him, so you boys don't get hurt."

Day after day, Pete waited for Flint Carter. He took care of the stallion and other horses. His face was swollen, he could barely see out of his left eye, and he could not eat solid foods. It was difficult to open or close his mouth. He had horrible headaches and it was hard for him to concentrate.

The storekeeper's wife thought Pete was dying, so she had a mountain man, Brock, take a look at him. The man said he was lucky. His jaw wasn't broken but it was dislocated, and he did have a cracked rib or two. He took a piece of leather, placed it under Pete's chin, brought it up around his jaws, and tied it on top of his head to keep his mouth from opening too far. Next, Brock wrapped cloth tight around his chest and said Pete needed to rest and get some better food if he was going to live. The storekeeper's wife secretly gave Pete a little soup and water each day. But she kept him chained to the post in the barn. At night Pete would crawl under the wagon or sleep with the horses to keep warm.

One night, he heard the storekeeper talking to a stranger.

"What's new?" he said. "How was your train ride down the mountain?"

"Fine! We did have a little excitement. That Carolyn, slave of that Miss Amy, died on the way. She had a stroke . . . so they said. The train stopped just long enough to put her in a shallow, unmarked grave along the railway. That train had a schedule to keep, and she was just a slave, so they had to keep moving."

"You don't say. She was a pretty woman with long brown hair. What a shame!"

"Any news here at Beck Spur?"

"Yes, that Flint Carter has been gambling and womanizing since he got here. Never seen a man who could drink so much liquor. He has lost five hundred to six hundred dollars. They are keeping him filled with drinks and taking his money little by little. You know that foolish man almost kilt his slave. I reckon that slave worth two thousand, five hundred dollars or more. Ben Brock, the mountain man, treated him and said he might make it if he is given half a chance.

Pete thought, he had never known of Carolyn having headaches. But Miss Amy did. She had them often. And she was wearing a dark black veil to cover her like Mrs. Eva wanted when she got on the train. Hence, no one could see her face. And Flint Carter had rented a small sleeping room for Miss Amy and Carolyn, so Miss Amy could lay down and rest. He knew Miss Amy had brown hair but he had never seen Carolyn's hair. Carolyn always had her hair covered. He wondered who was in the grave, Miss Amy or Carolyn. They looked so much alike. And it was rumored that they had the same father but different mothers. They were the same height and about the same weight—skin color too. The only thing that really made you know Carolyn was a slave was her clothing, the way she walked with her head hanging down, and how her hair was always covered in slave cloth. It seemed a little farfetched that both girls would have brown hair.

He silently hoped it was Miss Amy in the grave and not Carolyn. He wanted to believe that Carolyn was passing for white and free. If only he knew the color of Carolyn's hair, he could be certain who was in the grave.

Finally, after a week, Flint Carter returned to the barn and said, "Unchain that nigger. Hitch up the team, Pete. We are going back to Cross Junction while I got a little money left." Pete's muscles were sore and stiff because he had been shackled so long. His jaw was beginning to heal but he had extreme headaches each day. He was cold and was moving,- very slow. Flint Carter took out his bullwhip and gave him ten lashes across his back.

"This will teach you to move faster," he said. Pete clenched his fists but dared not look at him. He knew Flint Carter wanted an excuse to beat him. He said nothing, working to place blinders, bits, reins, a clocker, a back saddle, and a yoke on each horse. Next, he hooked up the trace and placed water in the water barrel and they were ready to go. He wondered if they were really going back to the plantation. And how were things at Round Pond Plantation?

The next two days were pure hell. Flint Carter would severely beat him for the smallest thing. His back was soaked in his own blood. He was not allowed hot food nor hot water. He sucked on herbs from his med bag to stay alive. Finally, when they stopped for the night on December 12, Flint Carter said, "We should be back at the plantation one or two days at most. Clean yourself and get some sleep. Wonder what is going on at the plantation? I bet Mrs. Eva is still the same."

Pete did not say a word but he wondered if his grandsons and daughter, Mariah, were safe. And he knew he had to try to escape from Flint Carter if he could.

CHAPTER FOURTEEN

Hurting Deep Within My Soul

The slave quarters were a buzz. Each day there seemed to be a new development. Mrs. Eva was worse than ever. She flogged slaves at a whim. When she saw Mossy Ella's newborn and how white it looked, she threw the babe into the hog-killing fire, calling the babe another bastard of Ed Smith. Strange, chilling cries, moans, and screams could be heard over the slave quarters as the babe died, yelling. Mothers, angels, spirits, and devils let out groans of inhuman sorrow and disbelief. Even the sky turned gray and then blue-black, and a chill swept through the plantation that could be felt by all. Mossy Ella filled her clothes with stones, walked into the river, and drowned.

No aid nor help had arrived from Mrs. Eva's father. Nor had Master Ed returned or sent word. As each day went by, Mrs. Eva realized how alone she was except for the three white overseer families who lived on the edge of the plantation. She could not abide the men or their wives. Nor did she want anything to do with their children. Poor white trash, she called them. And she had nothing in common with poor white trash. She could feel how much the slaves despised her. It was worse after that incident with Mossy Ella's baby. Why should they care? she thought. Even Old Sarah tried to avoid her. Hence, she kept her dogs and her guns at the ready, and hired four more men to police the plantation and make sure the slaves were watched and locked up nightly.

Each day she would sit on the second-floor veranda, awaiting news and watching for trouble. She handed out orders like a deranged military general and punished niggers and whites alike if she felt her orders were not obeyed.

On the morning of December 12, she was surprised that old Pete, Frank, and Flint Carter had not returned. What should have been a two-to-three-day trip had stretched into eight days or more.

Seven slaves ran for the freedom road. Three were caught and Mrs. Eva hanged them from three big oak trees on the hill in the north pasture. You could see that "bitter fruit" hanging for miles and miles. The smell of rotten human flesh was almost unbearable. Overseer Graves had come to her the day before and asked if the slaves could be taken down and buried.

"Hell no!" Mrs. Eva said. "They are going to hang there until the slave auction is over. Let it be a warning to any slave who runs for the freedom road that Mrs. Eva Smith from Round Pond Plantation will see a slave dead before she sees a slave free!"

"You are a hard woman, Mrs. Eva. Putting them in the ground would do no harm," he said.

"Nothing but bad luck and bad news keeps coming my way," said Mrs. Eva. "Now explain to me again what happened to my cotton, Overseer Graves."

"Like I said before, Mrs. Eva. The slaves picked all the cotton and it came to six hundred bales, five hundred pounds per bale. I had some of the slaves drive the cotton to market at Cross Junction. When we got there the sheriff was waiting and took them bales of cotton for debts owed by Master Ed. Ma'am, he said they mostly gambling debts and such. I told him that cotton was going for thirty cent a pound or more, and that six hundred bales by five hundred pounds by thirty cents would make our cotton worth ninety-thousand dollars! The sheriff said he was sorry. Mr. Ed signed an IOU against the cotton crop. He said you could come to town and plead your case before Judge Hargraves, but he did not think it would do you any good. What a powerful shame, six hundred bales of prime North Carolina cotton gone and this plantation did not receive a penny! How could Master Ed do such a thang?" said Graves.

"After the slave auction I will go into town and handle the problem. Do not worry."

"I am not Mrs. Eva, but—"

" But what?" she said.

"The men are wondering if they could have a little advance on their pay. Usually, we receive money after the cotton is sold. Under these circumstances—slave auction and all, Master Ed gone—you need to give the men a little something before they leave."

"Yes, I should," she said. "How about one thousand for you and five hundred each for the other three men—that is half of what they are owed. I will pay the balance after the slave auction with a bonus."

"That sounds fair, ma'am. A bonus, you say?"

"Good! Then it is settled," she said. "Now go and have all the slaves meet in front of the Big House. It is time for me to officially announce the slave auction."

"Yes, ma'am."

"Have them here at two p.m."

"Two it is," said Graves.

While Graves walked down the steps of the veranda, Eva noticed that Banker Overton, from Frost-Overton Bank, was coming up the plantation's magnolia-tree lined drive. He was dressed in his finest three-piece morning suit, complete with vest and top hat. He had a cigar hanging from his lips and was wearing fine Texas boots with a stylish bowler hat sporting a well-dressed slave driver who looked more royal than Overton ever could! Each time she had encountered the man he always reminded her of a beady-eyed weasel. Overton was a thief, like his father before him. And the only reason he would be coming to her home was to deliver bad news or to try to force her into a bad deal concerning the plantation.

She decided that she would not allow him to come in her house. He would see the denial as an afront to the station in life he was trying to achieve. When he pulled up to the veranda, she said, "Good morning, Overton," as if he was a hired hand. "What brings you out here on such a cold and miserable day?"

"Good Morning Eva," he said with a smirk. He called her by her given name to let her know she had come down a peg or two in the world. He meant it as an insult and she took it as such.

Laughing she said, "Now Mr. Overton, my brothers would be appalled that you were calling me by my given name. So that there is no misunderstanding I suggest you continue to call me Mrs. Eva or Mrs. Eva Smith, 'causes those boys are quick-tempered and faster on the trigger than I am," she said, holding her pistol in her hand. "We would not want my brothers to think you were trying to disrespect me."

Overton looked and saw Eva holding her gun and said, "No harm meant, Mrs. Eva."

"None taken, Overton. Now state your business!" said Eva.

"Well . . . I . . . I am here on behalf of the bank to make an inventory for the auction."

"What business has your bank to do with my auction? Anyway, that won't be necessary, Overton—Overseer Graves has already completed that task. We know how to conduct an auction!" Gun in hand, pointing to the trees where the slaves were hanging, she continued by saying, "But, you can find him on that hill yonder to the north, near that big oak tree grove. You won't miss it."

"Mrs. Eva, I also came out to present this payment demand letter for the mortgage on the plantation. Did you know Mr. Ed took out a mortgage on the land after he left for New Orleans? Anyway, it will be due on December fifteenth. Now the bank president says—"

Interrupting him and showing great irritation before he could utter another word she stood and firmly said, "You mean your father said what?"

"Well, Papa says if the mortgage is not paid on December fifteenth, you will... Well, will need to pack up and leave before Christmas. Do you understand!" he said loudly. Shaking, Overton leaned against a column on the porch.

"Hmm, would you know anything about the sheriff confiscating my cotton?" asked Eva.

"I heard about it, but I don't know any details," said Overton.

"I am told I have to see Judge Hargrave about the cotton. Am I wrong or isn't he your kin? Isn't he your mother's cousin?" He ignored her and said, "Mrs. Eva, I... I was wondering if you would allow me to go in the house and look at your things."

"What? MY THINGS!" she yelled.

He tried to gather himself and continued by saying, "I might want to purchase a thing or two at the auction tomorrow."

"Overton, understand: my personal things are not for sale. It is time for you to take your leave! You are welcome to come early on tomorrow morning to inspect the slaves. And I will be very, very, happy for my brothers to show you around. There seems to be some things you do not understand."

Then he said, "I am sorry, Mrs. Eva! Let's be frank, looks like you are going to lose almost everything. Why don't you sell the land to me and my papa and leave before the auction in the afternoon?"

" Isn't that illegal, sir?"

"No, it's legal—the land is in your name. And you have the right to sell most anything you like before the auction. After the auction, all proceeds will go to the creditors."

"Oh," she said, hanging her head slightly."

"I could fix everything," said Overton. "You wouldn't have to worry your pretty little head bout a thang. I know women do not have a head for business."

She smiled, batted her eyelashes with all the politeness and cunning of a true southern belle, and said, "That is something . . . um . . . to consider, Banker Overton. I was wondering how much money you would be willing to give me for the plantation. We have debts, I am told—or rather, Ed has debts. Well into the thousands. Give me a firm offer and time to think it over and I will get back to you before the auction at two p.m.," she said. "Now about the inventory, you go see Graves in the north pasture."

She stood, picked up his bowler hat, and gave it to him. Not knowing what to do, poor Overton ran down the stairs, turned the buggy around, and headed toward town. If he could get his hands on her land, he would not want to buy anything else Eva Smith owned. Mrs. Eva noted that he was not going to see Overseer Graves. Looks like he had lost interest in the inventory. He was not concerned about the slave prices nor money Ed owed. He wanted to buy her land. Why? She stood in the window and look down the road searching for her father, her husband, old Pete, Frank, and Flint Carter. But there was no one.

The word about the 2:00 p.m. meeting went through the slave community quickly. There was various rumor and speculations of the meeting. The slaves were used to meeting at the Big House for the announcement of important events like the birth of a master's child, deaths of the master's kin, or an allotment of clothing or shoes for the winter. Since they had worked extremely hard and taken twelve hundred bales of cotton to market some slaves thought they were going to get a small token of appreciation. Something simple—a day off, a good meal, lumber to repair the slave cabins, tar to seal their roofs, time to collect wood for the winter.

Others thought Mrs. Eva had word about Master Ed Smith. Or maybe she had come to herself and would allow the dead men hanging from the trees to be buried. No one except William, Daniel, Mariah, Old Sarah, and Jenny knew about the slave auction.

At 2:00 p.m. on December 13, 1860, more than 150 slaves, two overseers, four guards, Dr. Baker, and old Mrs. Williams, a white slave preacher, stood on the massive lawn of the Big House awaiting Mrs. Eva. A few minutes after 2:00 p.m., she appeared alone on the second floor of the veranda, dressed in one of her finest gowns, holding her fan to hide a pistol in her hand.

She said, "Good afternoon to you all. Change is coming! Change is coming! And we must be prepared! Before I start the meeting, I want all girls who have become women by having their first cycle come to the front and sit down on my left."

When China's little girl, Becca, began to move to the front, she put her hand on her arm and held her firmly, then looked to see if anyone noticed.

"And if you have just found out you are with child, come to the front and sit on my right.

We need to celebrate these life changes. Changes is coming, I tell you."

She smiled and waited until the girls and women were in place. Then she had Jenny give yellow cloth to the girls and red cloth to the expectant mothers.

She said, "Girls, please tie this cloth around your head and be sure you wear your new headcloth for the next few days."

Women and girls did as they were told and tied the scarves on their heads in typical slave style.

"Good," she exclaimed, "my, oh my! From up here, you look like a flower garden! Dr. Baker is here today and I know some of you have been feeling poorly. If you have not been well or you have body swelling, sores, boils, and such, go over to the wagon and wait for Dr. Baker. I will have him treat you today."

Next, she had old Mrs. Williams pray and read this passage from the Bible, "Ephesians six, verses five through six: Slaves be obedient to your masters, with fear and trembling and in sincerity of heart."

Ms. Williams added, "This Bible says if you slaves want to go to heaven, you got to happily obey Mrs. Eva and Mr. Ed, your masters, and work as hard as you can—hard as you can for them!" She pounded her hands on the Bible and said, "That is what it says right here in the good book."

Mrs. Eva walked to the middle of the second-floor veranda and said, "Dear ones, you have worked long and hard for the Round Pond Plantation! But our plantation has come on difficult times. There will be a slave auction day after tomorrow, December fifteenth, at two p.m. I have no choice in the matter! You need to try to look your best and be on your best behavior so you will go to a good home and be well fed. Of course, if you decide to become a hell-raiser and make trouble at the sale, you will be sold anyway but you will be bound for the mosquito rice fields, the deep delta of Mississippi, or the yellow fever swamps of Louisiana, where life will be harder and death is certain.

"Overseers and guards, thank you. Overseer Graves should have given you part of your pay. You will a receive the balance pay and a nice bonus after the auction.

"Slaves, I do have a heart. If possible, you will be sold as family."

A voice from the crowd asked, "Mrs. Eva, are you selling everybody? Are you gonna give anyone their freedom? Freedom that was promised? What will you do with Old Sarah and Grandma Emma?"

"No freedom papers for anyone! The plantation is on hard times—and yes, everyone must be sold, even Old Sarah and Grandma Emma," said Mrs. Eva, "You all will be put on the auction block day after tomorrow."

The slaves had mixed reactions: some cried, others fainted, many groaned and moaned. A few had no reactions at all; they just stared into space. Some men ripped their muscles so hard you could see their muscles moving under their clothes. Others smiled with clenched teeth but mostly the slaves looked trapped, lost, and betrayed. Mothers and fathers held their children as if they could protect them. They were all to be sold like a pig, horse, or cow to the highest bidder. And no matter what Mrs. Eva said, families would be sorted, separated, and sold to who paid her price!

"After this meeting, the guards will take you down to the river in small groups to bathed. Make sure you oil down your bodies with hog fat. Next you will see the overseers for inspection. If you pass the inspection you may go to your slave cabin and be with your family. All slaves that failed inspection because of age, illness, injury, or disease will be sent to Dr. Baker for a second chance to pass inspection. However, those slaves who do not pass this inspection will be taken and locked in the bargain hut. They will participate in the shooting games, or will be sold at a reduced sale price. They will not be allowed to leave the bargain hut or say goodbye to their families."

The slaves saw failing inspection as the worst fate a slave could have. Some of the older slaves knew what was involved in the "shooting games." Although it had never happened at Round Pond Plantation, a slave would be tied to an object and white men, white women, and sometimes their older white children would use slaves as target practice. They would bet to see who could shoot an object off a slave's head or hand or a specific body part. Some people would miss and the slave would be wounded. They would be awarded points for shooting off the slave's ears, putting out an eye, shooting off fingers and toes. The person with the greatest number of points would be declared the winner. The winner would then choose who would be allowed to deliver the killing shot to the slave's head or heart. When the slave died, they would jump up and down and shout, "Another free slave! Another free slave!"

Old white Mrs. Williams was the only person allowed to see slaves in the bargain hut and give their goodbyes to their slave families. Mrs. Williams would try to encourage these poor souls by saying, "If no one buys you, maybe you be set free."

Some of the slaves in the hut were encouraged by her words. Others tried to believe her, out of sheer desperation. A few knew their plight and thought only about the inhuman cruelty, humiliation, and death that awaited them and simply wanted the old white woman to be quiet. White Mrs. Williams would pray with each slave, hoping they would feel better. But when she tried to pray with old Grandma Emma, Emma said, "You mean well, but I is almost ninety-some odd years old. I can barely walk, or see, or take care of myself. I beg you to have mercy on me and my kin . . . bring me white oleander so I may brew a tea, a sweet-smelling apricot tea, pray to my Jesus, and meet him in glory without holes in my body in the morning!"

Mrs. Williams knew no one would buy an old, half-blind slave who could barely walk or take care of herself. She would be exactly what they would use for the games. But she said, "Emma, do not give up hope!"

"I didn't," said Emma. "Hope gave up on me. You and I both know Mrs. Eva ain't gonna let me live or be sold to someone else. She can't take the chance that I am not feeble-minded and won't reveal all of her secrets. I do not want to be a human target in one of her sick shooting games. Sadly," she said, "because I know her secrets, my life cannot be saved!"

Mrs. Williams knew Mrs. Eva had been a cruel child and grown up to be a horribly cruel woman who prided herself in saying, "I would rather see a slave dead, than to see a slave free." So, she asked God for forgiveness and gave Emma one of the small bags she had in her apron pocket. The bag smelled like apricots.

Emma took the bag and said, "Thank you for the oleander . . . white oleander."

Ms. Williams hugged Emma and left the hut.

As promised, Mrs. Eva allowed healthy slaves to go to their cabins to get warm and spend the night with their families. But she demanded that they wash and dry their clothes by morning—not because she wanted them clean, but because the nights were near freezing and it would be very hard to run for freedom in wet clothing on such a winter night.

She warned the slaves there would be guards on the plantation and anyone who was out after dark without permission would be punished. Anyone caught trying to run away or helping others running to the freedom road would be hung from the nearest tree.

As Mrs. Williams was going back to the Big House, Walter Spade yelled, "Wait up, Mrs. Williams. I want to ask you a question or two."

"No problem, Walter, what do you want to know? And why are you here—I have never known anyone in your family to be in the slave trade."

"Well, we have fallen on hard times, Ms. Williams, and a man got to try and make a living."

"I guess so," she said. "It is cold out here, baby, what do you want to know?"

"I want to know about the yellow and red scarfs."

"Oh!" she said. "Well, during a slave auction, yellow cloth is given to girls who have just had their first period. The cloth indicates that they are ready to be a breeder and have children, but they are still virgins. These girls, usually eleven to thirteen years old, will fetch high prices at the slave auction. And some of the prettier light-skinned girls are often sold to cathouses and their virginity sold to the highest bidder. It also warns buyers that they are not allowed to sample the merchandise without paying the slave's full price to the owner. Men are attracted to virgins of any color and are willing to pay top dollar to be their first sexual partner.

"The red cloth indicates that the slave is with child and a buyer is getting two for the price of one. This is a sad business, son. A lot of cruel, unspeakable things will happen between now and December fifteenth. Are you sure you want to be in the slave business?" Spade nodded his head. "Well stay alert and watch everyone—white and black alike."

He said, "Yes ma'am," and returned to his post near the barn.

As daylight turned to darkness, doom and sadness fell over the plantation like a hailstorm, bringing mountains of hurt and sorrow. Daniel and William were very fearful. Both boys tried not to cry! They had not seen their mother when the slaves gathered in front of the Big House, nor had they seen her at the river. It was rumored that Mrs. Eva was selling slaves in small groups and killing others. Could she be with Dr. Baker for a second inspection? Or, God forbid, was she in the bargain hut for some unknown reason?

Finally, they were allowed to go to the small room inside the barn. They made sure they were alone. Then, they began to talk quietly about the people who were missing. They wondered where was Old Grand Papa Pete and Frank. Then there was Leroy, Big Bertha, and several other men and women they knew and had not seen for days. In all they counted fifteen to twenty slaves who were missing. Were they alive or dead? Or were they in the bargain hut? Had they been sold? Where were Mrs. Eva's folks? That telegram said they were on their way to Cross Junction before Thanksgiving!

They were heating water to have some tea when suddenly there was a loud knock on the door. The guard Walter Spade said, "Overseer Graves has ordered you to come to the Big House PDQ—pretty dam quick."

When they saw Graves on their way to the Big House, he said Old Sarah was ill.

"Go and help Jenny at the Big House. Be quick!"

The boys ran to the kitchen of the Big House. Jenny sent them to pump tocarry water so she could do the wash and cook extra food for the Slave Auction.

As they were filling the large washpots and buckets with water, a wagon loaded with ten to fifteen slaves stopped at the well. The driver said, "Fill the barrel with water, boys." They looked into the wagon and chained to the floor they saw their mother. No one had to tell them. They knew she had been sold!

Mariah had been badly beaten. Bloodstains were on the cloth that covered her head and drops of blood ran down the corner of her mouth and fell onto her white apron. They wanted to run and hug her! Help her! To kill who dared to hurt their mother. But she tilted her head, lifted it, and met their eyes with a warning glance and they did not move! They stood frozen, like statues.

Finally, the driver said, "Hurry up, boys. I got to get these slaves on the boat to New Orleans. It's leaving tonight."

They finished the chore and watched the wagon as it rolled past them, down the driveway, out onto the main road, and deeper into the dark hellhole called slavery. Tears filled their eyes and silent cries leaped from their souls! They feared that they would never see their mother again. She would be lost in distance and time.

Where in the world was New Orleans? Daniel wondered. Was it in North Carolina? What kind of God would allow their mother to be treated so badly? Where was God's mercy, that mercy the preacher talked about in Bush Harbor on Sunday mornings. He knew he would forever be grateful to Overseer Graves because he had allowed him to see his mother—maybe for the last time!

CHAPTER FIFTEEN

Bitter Fruit

DECEMBER 14, 1860

At last, they were near the Round Pond Plantation. Old Grand Papa Pete drove the team as Flint Carter laid in the back of the wagon drinking a cheap "red eye." Pete was glad to be close to the plantation. He prayed that his child, Mariah, and his grandchildren, Daniel and William, were well. And he was still alive to see them.

Opening and closing his mouth was still extremely painful, his ribs were sore, and he knew his back was infected. At the plantation, he hoped the boys would have some pennyroyal he could use for pain. He could also use some sumac for his eye. He announced, "We be at the plantation in a few minutes, Mr. Carter."

Carter said, "Stop the wagon and let me get on my horse."

Pete stopped the wagon and saddled the stallion for Flint Carter. Pete noticed the stallion was uneasy, but he did not understand why.

Carter said, as he got on the horse, "If I wasn't so drunk, I would shoot you right here. And Pete, if you value your life, you will not say a word about Frank or what I did to you to Mrs. Eva."

Pete nodded, got back into the wagon, and drove it down the road toward the plantation.

At last, he was at his beloved Round Pond Plantation—the only home he had ever known. He did not announce their arrival with the *ghee gee* yell, as he usually did. As he drove down the lane, he noticed none of the slaves were out working. The horses were in the south pasture. Why weren't the horses in the north winter pasture, like they should be?

The stallion was skittish. The horse hesitated, snorted, refused commands, and was hard to control. It almost threw Flint Carter to the ground. Then the wind blew and he smelt a dead, rotting thing. It was upsetting the stallion and the dogs. What a stench—what animal or animals had died? Why hadn't they been buried or burned? Then he realized that what he smelt was flesh—dead human flesh! Rotten human flesh! He looked in the direction of the smell, lifted his head, looked toward the hill, and saw the "bitter fruit"—dead slaves, swinging in the oak trees. He could not recognize who the slaves were, but he knew that they must be his friends, his family, and maybe his distant kin! His beloved Round Pond Plantation was in turmoil!

Mrs. Eva's heart leaped for joy when she saw Pete and Flint Carter coming up the lane. When Pete did not yell to announce their arrival, she was annoyed! That yell was a plantation tradition. How dare he not yell and announce that they were back.

Was something wrong? she thought. She had smelt the dead slaves for so many days that the odor did not bother her, or perhaps mentally she ignored it. The rotten smell from the dead slaves was nothing like the rotten smell of her lousy marriage! And it was a warning to the slaves that she would track them down and kill anyone who tried to flee. She kept going over in her mind how she had gotten here, in this horrible situation. Where was her no-good husband? She could feel herself losing control. Her brain felt like it would explode. She was about to snap and hurt someone. She sat down, caressed the pistol in her hand, and took a minute to compose herself. Then she stood and got ready to receive them.

When they pulled up to the veranda, Flint Carter jumped down from his horse and said, "God, Eva, do something about that smell! Good God woman, how can you stand it?"

She ignored him, adjusted her pearls, and asked sweetly, "How was the trip? What happened?"

Flint Carter looked at her in disbelief and realized that Eva was as crazy as he had been told and said, "Well, there was a tornado in Camden. That little settlement is no more! I ain't never seen nothing like it. Every building was destroyed. Trees uprooted from the ground. That storm threw some people into the treetops. Only five people survived. Even the riverboat was smashed on the rocks into small pieces. I thought we would have to come back. But we found out about a new railroad line. We took your sister, Amy, to Beck Spur and put her on the train. We even paid a little more for an enclosed space on the train called a sleeping car so Amy could have some privacy and sleep. She is going to arrive in style."

"Oh! Thank God," said Mrs. Eva. "Where is Frank? Where is my Frank?" she asked.

"Well, we lost him, Mrs. Eva."

"Lost him!" she yelled. "How? How can you lose a grown man worth nearly two thousand dollars?"

Her eyes rolled back in her head as she waved her pistol. Carter stepped back for a moment and became completely sober. He had forgotten how crazy Eva could be.

Quietly he repeated, "We lost Frank, Eva."

"And what happened to my Pete? How did Pete get so badly hurt? Look at his face! Pete, can you see out of your left eye? I can't get top dollar for him hurt like that. He can't build the buildings on the plantation I need if he can't see. Why hell! He built this grand plantation house. What's wrong with you, Carter!"

Flint Carter lowered his voice, gave a warning glance at Pete, and spoke firmly, "As I said, Eva, we had trouble. Tornado and such? Can we talk in private?"

"All right," said Eva. "Like to see you explain to me why I should be out of five thousand dollars or more! Pete, drive around to the kitchen and have Old Sarah look at you. See if someone can drive the wagon to the barn and take care of the horses, if you ain't able."

Then as if a sweet switch had turned on in her brain, she said, "Thank you, Flint Carter! I love it when a man takes charge and gets a job done. Let me get your pay. The slave auction is tomorrow! Did you remember?" And with that they went into the parlor.

Pete drove around to the kitchen. Jenny exclaimed, "What happened to you, Grand Papa Pete?"

"Flint Carter has almost kilt me," he said.

"Come over by the fire and I will try to get you fixed up a little."

"Can you have someone drive the wagon to the barn and take care of the horses? I almost did not make it back," said Pete. "The only thing that kept me alive was thinking about Mariah and my boys. Have the boys come and help me!"

"That is not a good idea. It is not safe here at the Big House. Mrs. Eva is unpredictable! She even threw a baby into the hog-killing fire. I am going to fix your bandage on your head, and then I want you to go to the barn and wait for me with the boys. If anyone asked you tell them we are family: me, you, Sarah, Daniel, and William.

"And Mariah," he said.

"No, do as I say, Pete. I will tell you about Mariah when I come. All slaves are permitted to spend this last night with their family. I may be very late, but I will come."

Pete gathered all the strength he had and drove the wagon to the barn. He could barely get down from the wagon and go inside. Manny saw how hurt he was and said, "Grand Papa Pete let me take care of those horses. Go and try to get some rest. I will send for Daniel and William to help you."

Pete made his way to his little cot in the tiny room and that was the last thing he remembered.

When Daniel and William saw Pete's wagon, they were overjoyed. They hurried and finished their chores. Then ran to the barn looking for Old Grand Papa Pete. When they entered their small little room, they saw their grandfather lying almost lifeless on the bed, burning up with fever. William began to cry when Manny said, "Stop—he ain't dead but him powerful hurt."

Daniel ran to get help. Overseer Graves stopped him and said, "Boy what is the matter?"

"It is grand Papa Pete—he is bad off. I think he might die."

"Hush," Graves warned, "anyone sick has to go to the bargain hut and that means almost certain death. Let me take a look at him."

When Graves saw how bad Pete was hurt, he could not believe it. At first glance he saw that his jaw was broken or dislocated, his left eye was swollen shut, and he was burning up with fever.

"William, go and get some fresh water. Boil some water as well. Daniel, go to the kitchen in the Big House and tell Jenny I said to send some cloth for bandages and a towel. Tell her I want a bottle of whiskey for myself. And after she has finished with her chores, I want her to come to the barn. Do not let Mrs. Eva hear this, do you understand!"

"Yes sir," he said, and ran to the Big House

"Manny, do you know what to do for fever?"

"No sir, Grand Papa Pete is the slave doctor here. Maybe he told the boys what to do, or perhaps Jenny or Old Sarah know what to do."

"What do you think is causing this high fever?" asked Graves. "Help me take off his shirt and pants . . . let's look and see if something bit him."

First, they checked his feet and legs. All looked well. Then they removed his coat. Graves gasped at the smell. He had been treated harshly and with such brutality.

Pete has been beaten repeatedly with a whip that had metal barbs or glass attached. His back was covered with whip marks and punch holes left by the whip. He also had large boils on his shoulders. He looked as if someone had carved holes in his shoulder as a form of punishment.

Graves shook Pete and asked, "Who did this? Who did this?"

Pete was out cold and could not answer. He had bled so much that his shirt was stuck to parts of his body. Some of the holes were red. Other areas on his back were dark and oozing with pus, maggots, and debris. They placed Pete on his stomach and looked hopelessly at him.

"Manny, I do not know if he is going to make it. Wash his back and clean him up the best you can. After the wounds are clean pour the liquor over the wounds to disinfect them. Hopefully, Jenny will be here soon."

"Do you know where Pete has been?"

"No sir. He and Mr. Flint Carter just returned today. About two weeks ago Pete, Frank, and Mr. Flint went on an errand for Mrs. Eva."

"Oh!" said Graves, and started to leave the room.

"Do you think Dr. Baker can help?" asked Manny.

"I do not think so. Last time I saw him he was almost drunk at Mrs. Eva's dinner party. Let's keep this between us as long as we can. I do not want to take a chance of Pete going to the bargain hut."

William returned with the water. He felt how hot his grandfather was and said, "Manny, lift him up and help me get some medicine in him. It will help with the fever."

"OK," said Manny. "I need something to wash him. We do not even have a clean rag or soap."

"Use anything!" said William, "We got to try."

They soaked Pete's shirt with warm water to remove it. Daniel returned with the bandages, towel, and whiskey. He took some horse chestnut seeds, placed them in water, rubbed them together, and soon there was a little soap to clean poor Pete.

"William, we must remember every medicine and things Grand Papa Pete taught us— maybe we can save him. Jenny cannot come until after Mrs. Eva stops entertaining and goes up to bed."

"I gave him some of that boneset for the fever. But he is still burning up. Make a plaster with sage. We will put it on his chest and that will also help. Our big problem is what's causing the fever. All of these boils and infected areas on his back must be drained and clean."

"If that is the case, boys, it is best we do that while he is out cold," said Manny. "That is going to be very painful."

"We need a knife with a sharp point. We have to lance these sores."

"How?" asked William.

"Like we lanced the sores on the pigs and horses," said Daniel.

"There are so many of them. We need help," said William.

"No matter! Help may not come. We cannot wait on Aunty Jenny. We can only depend on ourselves to get this job done. All right," said Manny, "I have a couple of knives I use on the horses."

They took the knives, washed them, and put the knives into the fire to get them red hot. After the knives cooled, they began. Daniel would lance a sore and William would push on it to get out the pus and debris. Sometimes the pus was white, other times it was yellow, or green. The sores smelled horrible. But they kept going until they got to the sores on his shoulder. They were the size of hen eggs, and one of them had maggots.

Daniel lanced the first one and pus, blood, and maggots shot across the room. Manny took a sip of the whisky and said not a word. Next, they tried the second one. It was hot and rock hard. William said, "This one is different. It looks like Grand Papa Pete has had this one a long time. Do you think we should bother it?"

"Yes, because it is hot. It is probably causing a lot of the fever. It has to go."

"Boys, since this one is different, clean that knife again before you start," instructed Manny.

"All right," they said.

"While you clean the knife, I will see if Old Pete has a fish needle and some thread. We are gonna have to sew up some of these areas," said Manny.

After the knife cooled again, Daniel lanced the boil. William pushed on the area but only a little blood came out. But William could feel something hard inside. Then Daniel cut a little deeper and out came pus and then shotgun pellets. They counted five pellets in all. Manny poured whisky in the wound, took the fish needle, and sewed up this wound and several others.

"Why are you sewing him up?" asked the boys.

"That's what white people do when they get shot or when they have a big cut. What is good for them is good for us," he said. "Well boys . . . I think we have done all we can. I am going to be with my wife and kids. It may be the last time I get to see them. Let him sleep! But he must be ready for the slave auction tomorrow. It starts at two. Do not tell anyone how bad he is hurt. You do not want Old Grand Papa Pete to go to the bargain hut. That hut should be called the death hut. Boys, you need to get some sleep and rest. Make yourselves a bit of food. Tomorrow will be a long day. Ain't no telling when you have your next meal."

"Manny, have you ever been sold at an auction?"

"Yes, William I have. It is one of the worst things a man can do to another. Keep your faith in God." Manny hugged both boys and said, "Good night."

Jenny could not get away until the supper and dishes were done. Mrs. Eva and Mr. Flint Carter were having dinner with several men who were slave buyers. After dinner the men went back to town, stating they would return for the slave auction at two, and Flint Carter went with them. Mrs. Eva had a little too much to drink and went upstairs to bed. Finally, the house was quiet.

Old Sarah went to the door of the kitchen and called the guard and asked him if he would like some of her good coffee and a slice of cake and if he would allow Jenny to spend the night with her family in the barn. He agreed. Jenny took a basket with food, clothing for Pete, and medicine, and went to the barn. The guard came into the kitchen to get warm and to eat the food that was promised.

CHAPTER SIXTEEN

Just Before Dawn

DECEMBER 15, 1860

It was close to 1:00 a.m. when Jenny entered the barn and went to Pete's room. The boys were asleep and Pete was lying on his stomach recovering from his beatings. She looked at his body and realized that Pete was not an old man—he might be in his mid-forties. He was a well-built man! His oversized clothes hid what a fine body he had. He was tall, with broad shoulders, a thin waist, and narrow hips. The color of his skin always reminded her of sweet caramel. She thought that if they were free, Pete would make a fine husband. And she would run him to ground until he agreed to marry her!

She pushed these thoughts out of her mind and covered the boys with a blanket. She checked Pete and found he had a fever. She heated some water and made him a hot toddy.

"Here, wake up, Pete. Wake up, Pete, and drink this!"

He opened his eyes for a minute and drank the liquid and went back to sleep. In his sleep he mumbled her name and said, "I love you, Jenny." She attributed his words to his high fever. Jenny brewed some coffee and kept cold compresses on Pete's head and under his arms. She made a stew and placed it on the fire to cook for tomorrow's meal. Finally, she sat on a quilt by Pete's cot and fell asleep.

Around 3:00 a.m., she felt someone stroking her hair. It was a firm, gentle stroke—a loving stroke. For a moment she thought she was dreaming. The hand touched her face and a finger ran across her lips and then she opened her eyes to see Pete. He smiled and said, "Thank you! Thank you, my sweet Jenny!"

Jenny was so shocked by Pete's actions and words. She could not say a thing.

"I have loved you, Jenny, for a long time but I have never had the heart to say so. What does a slave have to offer a beautiful woman like you? Not even a name. I only have the white man's name. But I remember my family's African name is Odilli. I know I have waited too long to tell you that I love you. Tomorrow, we may be sold and never see each other again. But I have hope. So, I give my heart and soul to you, Jenny." He stood and said, "I ask that you marry me, here and now, and become the wife of Peter Odilli!"

She smiled and said, "Oh, Pete!"

He took her hand and said, "I, Peter Odilli, do take Jenny as my wife, in the midst of slavery and in the hope of freedom. I promise to love her beyond these walls of time and despair."

"Oh, Peter!"

"Well girl, will you marry me or not!"

They laughed and she said, " I do. I do, you sweet-talking thang."

He sat on the cot and said, "Climb in the bed with me, girl. Let me hold you for a while."

"You cannot hold me, Pete; you are badly hurt."

"Then you hold me, Jenny."

He climbed off the cot and laid next to Jenny on the floor. Neither of them said a word. They held, touched and loved each other and soon they were making love to each other with all of their being. Jenny did not know if Pete was making love to her out of need, love, or despair— maybe all three. She didn't care! She was lost in a vast ocean of hot caramel-chocolate arms and legs, mind melting lava kisses, and a longing for a man like she had never had before. Peter Odilli made every inch of her body come alive. She felt things she had never experienced. She knew she had lost her mind and she had no intentions of trying to find it. Pete kept saying, "I have always loved you, Jenny." Tears of joy ran down her face as they stole moments of happiness and unspeakable joy. She thanked God for allowing her to be truly loved by someone.

Near daybreak, Pete said, "Jenny, I wish things were different. I wish we were free and had a home of our own."

"Oh! Pete, what are we going to do?"

"Think! Think! And try to be sold as a family," said Pete.

"Mrs. Eva will never allow it. She would not even allow Miss Amy to take me with her. Mrs. Eva said she needs me, and Miss Amy took Carolyn."

"How do you know that?"

"Old Sarah and I listened to Miss Amy and Mrs. Eva through the stovepipe in the dining room when they were upstairs."

"Well, Jenny, tell me what has been going on at the plantation while I was away. Tell me about Mariah, the slave auction. Do you know where Master Ed is? And where are the people that Mrs. Eva's papa said he would send? Who is Flint Carter?"

"All right, let me make some coffee and I will tell you what I know."

"Start with Mariah," he said.

"OK," she said slowly. "Mrs. Eva sold Mariah and twelve more slaves to a buyer from New Orleans. At first Mariah was not a part of the deal. But she found out Mrs. Eva was selling slaves off before the auction and she had sold about fifteen teenage boys to Master Brown—you know the one who likes to sleep with men—while she was working at the Anderson Plantation. Master Brown had one of the boys from our plantation over to the Anderson place and he and the Anderson men were demonstrating 'buck breaking.' The poor lad was not allowed a belt nor a piece of rope to keep up his pants. He had to wear his pants down with part of his butt always showing. Mr. Brown, Lonnie Anderson and a few of the other men would have the boy bend over and they would bang the boy from behind. The boy would fight, scream, and try to run away! So they tied the boy to a table and took turns raping him. It was a game! This went on all night.

"The next morning when Mariah went to work, she saw the boy. He was begging for help; blood was running from his behind. He said, 'Aunty Mariah, please help me get away.' She brought the boy some water and a rag. Brown heard the boy tell Mariah that Mrs. Eva had sold him and fourteen more boys from our plantation to Brown and he was raping everyone.

"Mariah completed her day and returned here. Brown came to the plantation shortly after. Mrs. Eva called Mariah to the Big House and asked her what the boy said. When Mariah lied and said she could not understand him, Brown hit her so hard that blood ran from her head and mouth and then he beat her with a whip."

Pete held his head in his hands and began to cry. Jenny stopped talking.

"Go on—please go on," he said.

"Mrs. Eva kept Mariah locked in the pantry for two days. On the day the man came to pick up the slaves for New Orleans, she sold Mariah as well. She told me and Old Sarah, she would kill us if we told anyone."

"Any word about Master Ed?"

"No, not a word."

"Or Mrs. Eva's family?"

"No. Nobody has come to help her. Banker Overton came and gave her a demand letter about a mortgage that Master Ed was to have taken out on the plantation the day he left for New Orleans. The only person who has come to help her is that that Flint Carter. But he is a snake— worse than Mr. Ed if you asked me. I've never seen him do it, but I think he slaps her around. He has some hold on her. He is nothing but POOR WHITE TRASH. He cannot even eat properly at a table—using nothing but his spoon, never a fork like a proper gentleman. And Mrs. Eva cannot stand poor white trash. So… he must have some kind of hold on her."

"Jenny, what did you and Old Sarah pack in the crates that Frank and I took to Camden."

"Mostly all the valuable things she had in this house—the silver and gold dishes, crystal, china, copper pots, linens, and rugs. Old Sarah and I heard her tell Miss Amy that she had sewn their mother's diamonds, pearls, and some money in her jacket."

"Jenny, when you go back to the Big House listen and try to find out what you can."

"All right . . . Pete, you know all women can be jealous, and I am no different. I couldn't help but notice when I came here with Mrs. Eva six years ago that you and Mariah were close.

Was she your wife before me?"

Pete laughed. "No, my pretty! No need to worry! Mariah is my daughter. William and Daniel are my grandsons. But do not tell anyone this. If you do, it could mean the boys' lives."

"I won't," she said.

Sweet-smelling coffee and the aroma of the soup filled the room.

"Let me get you something to eat, Pete. And we need to do something about your eye." Pete was starved and he ate the food with delight and added a sumac spice to help the swelling in his body and eye.

"Here are some clean clothes I got for you. Put these on."

He put on the clothes, walked over, and kissed Jenny.

"Jenny, I will always love you," he said. "Always!"

"What happened to you, Pete?" asked Jenny.

"Flint Carter sold Frank to a lady from Camden called Mrs. Burns. When I said he had no right to sell Frank, he hit me with the trace and stomped me and kicked in my ribs. Then he decided to stay in Camden to drink and gamble. Each day there I got a beating. If it had not been for a mountain man called Brock, I would not have made it."

"What happened to Carolyn and Miss Amy?"

"I am not sure . . . but one of them is dead. You know Carolyn could pass for white. I was chained to a post in the barn and I heard the storekeeper and a stranger talking. The stranger said Carolyn had died on the train and they had buried her by the side of the railway without even a marker. He said it was a shame, and how the slave Carolyn had long, pretty brown hair."

"Brown hair, did you say?" ask Jenny.

"Yes, brown hair. So, since I didn't know the color of Carolyn's hair, I wasn't quite sure who was dead—Miss Amy or Carolyn. Do you know the color of Carolyn's hair?"

Before she could answer there was a knock on the door. Pete opened the door to find a half-frozen, portly, strange, rich-looking white gentleman who asked if he could come in.

"I'm looking for Pete. I hope he can treat my horse. I am John Francis Bernard Kaufman from Tennessee."

"I am Pete."

" Pete, you may not remember me but you treated and cured some of my horses four or five years back on the Sandusky Place."

"Now I remember," said Pete. "I will be glad to help you."

"Here is a cup of coffee," said Jenny. "Black is all I can offer. It will warm you up a mite."

He brushed the ice out of his mustache and said, "Thanks ma'am. If you don't mind, could I have a bowl of your stew as well? It smells real-good and I am powerful hungry. I have been riding all night and I haven't eaten in a day or so."

"Why of course you can," said Pete. "Why, my Jenny is the best cook in these parts."

"This is some of the best coffee I have ever had," said Mr. Kaufman. "Strong and black—the way I like it."

"Stay here and warm up while I look at your horse."

"Wait and I will go with you," said Mr. Kaufman as he gobbled down the soup. "Mighty fine food! Mighty fine. Pete, I bet your wife could work wonders with a well-stocked kitchen.".

"That she could," agreed Pete.

"It is the chestnut mare. I am not sure what is wrong. I would sure hate to lose that horse. She is with a foal. We were returning from the horse races in New Orleans and I was trying to get home before she foals."

"Let's get her in the barn and see what is wrong. Jenny, wake the boys. I will need their help," said Pete.

Pete looked at the horse and saw that the horse was bloated and very pregnant. The horse was in pain, trying to bite its flanks, pawing at the ground, not drinking its bucket of water and stretching as it urinated.

"Mr. Kaufman, has your horse been eating lately?"

"No not really, Pete."

"Having a poop?"

"No," he said.

"Mr. Kaufman, your horse has the colic. Colic in a horse is very dangerous and you may have to put down this horse."

"What causes colic, Pete?"

"Well," said Pete, "dryness or coarseness of food or a bile blockage, grain overload, sand ingestion, or parasite infection. Any off these things can cause colic. You know, some jockeys will give rival horses sand so that they will develop colic and cannot race. If I get started right away, maybe we can save this horse. Mr. Kaufman, I belong to Mr. Ed and Mrs. Eva Smith. They are having a slave auction here today at two. Mrs. Eva is selling everyone. I can only promise to help you until I and my family are sold."

"Do not worry about that Pete. I will buy you and your family at auction, if you can save the horse. At any rate, I appreciate what you can do. This mare is carrying the foal of an Arabian stallion. She is part Arabian herself. I would hate to lose her foal. Pete, have you ever seen an Arabian stallion?"

"Well sir, I had not until about three weeks ago. A man named Flint Carter, a friend of Mrs. Eva, has one. He is new to these parts. It is a beautiful animal."

"Would you happen to know where this Carter lives?" asked Mr. Kaufman.

"No sir, but he will be here today for the auction." Pete saw no need to tell Mr. Kaufman that when he first saw the horse it belonged to a free black man. He wasn't even sure that the black man was gone from Ms. Cooper's house. It was in his best interest to give just enough information but not to tell all he knew. "Well sir, the boys and I have got to get started. What is the name of your horse?"

"Kitty Two."

"That is a funny name for a horse."

"Yes, it is. My son named this mare Kitty Two and the stallion Kitty."

"Daniel and William, walk this horse until I come back with some medicine for it. Do not let the horse lay down. Rub her sides."

Mr. Kaufman sat down and watched the boys work with the horse.

"You boys seemed to be very skilled with horses."

"Yes sir, we are," said Daniel. "Old Grand Papa Pete, William, and me make money treating sick horses and animals all over the countryside."

Mr. Kaufman looked in his saddle bags and took out some newspapers.

"Here are the latest newspapers from New Orleans," he said. "Can you boys read?"

"No sir," said Daniel. "But we like hearing stories."

He picked up a newspaper and began to read articles to the boys as they work and showed them pictures of people and places in New Orleans. About 6:00 a.m. he said, "I think I will go up to the Big House and share these papers with Mrs. Eva and get a little more breakfast."

Mr. Kaufman gathered the papers, walked up the hill, and knocked on the front door. Jenny answered it and invited him in.

"Tell Mrs. Eva that John Francis Bernard Kaufman is here and that I was sent by her father."

"Yes sir," said Jenny and ran up the stairs.

Mrs. Eva was battling a hangover and a black eye. But when Jenny announced that help had come from her father, she got up and ran down the stairs. She greeted Mr. Kaufman and said she would be back down as soon as she got dressed.

"Jenny, give Mr. Kaufman breakfast; I will be back downstairs in a few minutes."

Jenny asked Mr. Kaufman to wait in the parlor but he followed her in the kitchen and began eating the biscuits and sorghum syrup she had prepared for breakfast.

"What are they building out front?" he asked.

"It is a platform for the slave auction," she said sadly.

"Oh! I see," said Mr. Kaufman. "Why are you cooking so much food? Look at these cakes, pies, roast pig, and the like."

"Mrs. Eva is expecting Banker Overton and his son, Mr. Flint Carter, Dr. Baker, Ms. Cooper, Pastor Roberts, Overseer Graves, the telegraph man, Mr. Roberts, Mr. Gamble, the auctioneer, and several others for lunch at 11:30 a.m."

"What are they meeting about?"

"I do not know, sir."

"How did Pete get hurt so badly?"

"Well sir Mrs. Eva sent him on a trip with Flint Carter and he came back that way. Sir, how would you like your eggs: scrambled or over easy?"

"Over easy," he said.

On an oversized plate she put ham, cheese grits, and eggs. She filled a smaller plate with biscuits, butter, and jam.

"Come and eat in the dining room while Mrs. Eva gets ready, sir.'"

Thank you, I will. Jenny, do not forget to bring me some coffee and a big piece of cake. I'd like to try that chocolate one. I love to eat good food," he said, as he sat down and began eating.

In the barn, Pete made a tonic for the horse. He used dandelion to boost digestion, valerian root as a sedative to relieve some of the cramps and constipation, meadowsweet to help relieve pain, peppermint to help relieve the colic, and garlic to boost digestion. He placed the items in a pot, added water, and boiled them for almost thirty minutes. While the mixture cooled, he chopped several cloves of garlic and hand fed them to the horse. He talked to the horse as if she was a human lady. He had the boy drape blankets over the horse to keep her warm.

Next, he and Manny took a funnel and forced the liquid down the horse's throat.

"We will have to force this liquid down the horse every hour," he said.

Daniel, William, and Pete took turns walking the horse and Pete and Manny gave the horse its tonic every hour.

"Well, we will know in about two to three hours if this horse can be saved. While we wait, boys, go and pack as many dry herbs as you can for horses and men. Get the nuts we gathered for winter. Pack our blankets and quilts. There is still a slave auction today and we have to be ready."

It took Mrs. Eva about an hour to get ready and come downstairs. Before she came down stairs, she went to the second-floor veranda and saw that the platform had been built for the slave auction and was pleased that all was in order. Her papa had sent help—this was going to be a great day! She got her pistol, placed it in her handbag, attached the handbag to her waist, and walked down the stairs.

When she entered the dining room Mr. Kaufman stood and said, "I am John Francis Bernard Kaufman and I am here to assist you on behalf of your father, brothers, and cousins. Here is your father's ring so you will know what I say is true."

She took the ring and examined it.

"Have a seat sir, please sit down."

"Mrs. Eva, I have known your father for many years. I want to talk to you before the auction and show you some news articles. It is clear to me that all is not right here. Someone or a few people have gotten together to take advantage of you.

"First, Ed Smith is dead! He died before he got to New Orleans. Hence, it is impossible for him to have accumulated gambling debts in New Orleans."

Eva flopped down in her chair and was speechless for a moment. Then she screamed, "Ed is dead!"

"My dear, you must get a hold of yourself," said Mr. Kaufman. "I think we should move to the upstairs parlor. I have much to tell you. I am going to have Jenny bring you some coffee and bourbon and some food. What you decide and do in the next few hours will determine your wealth and hence your future. I want you to give orders to bury those dead run-a-away slaves. We have a lot to discuss before the auction. Compose yourself—I do not want the slaves to know what we are discussing."

The news that Ed Smith, her husband, was dead was almost more than she could comprehend. She indeed was sad that he was dead but happy to be free of the marriage!

"Jenny! Jenny!" she screamed. "Take some coffee, bourbon, cake, and breakfast food to the upstairs parlor. Then go and find Overseer Graves and have him bury those slaves on the hill before ten a.m. If anyone comes before we come down, just have them wait in the parlor and feed them."

"Yes ma'am," said Jenny.

Jenny took a tray up the stairs filled with goodies Mrs. Eva had requested. Next, she hurried and told Overseer Graves that Mrs. Eva wanted the runaway slaves buried before 10:00 a.m. Overseer Graves said, "Thank God almighty, she has finally come to her senses."

On her way back to the Big House kitchen she heard crying and moaning—the slave telegraph said Grandma Emma had died in her sleep. She bowed her head and walked slowly back to the kitchen to complete her chores. She was going to miss Grandma Emma. She would have loved to tell her that she and Pete were married—married the only way they could be.

Slowly, she climbed the stairs leading to the kitchen and went into the dining room to clear the breakfast table only to catch Old Sarah listening at the stovepipe. "One of these days you are going to get caught," she said quietly.

"Listen, listen, "said Old Sarah. "Mrs. Eva been crying since you left. I want to find out what that is about. That evil child don't cry for nothing."

Jenny went to listen at the stovepipe and she had Sarah to watch the door.

"Now stop that crying! I know you did not love Ed. Smith," said Mr. Kaufman. "Your marriage was just a business transaction."

"All right," said Mrs. Eva, "please tell me again."

Mr. Kaufman was almost shouting when he said, "Ed Smith is dead! He died before he arrived in New Orleans. He died on the Mississippi Bell on November fifth. I know one should not speak ill of the dead, but your husband was a snake. He was going to New Orleans to marry a socialite, a Miss Suzanne Clayton. When he died an article was placed in the paper giving notice that their wedding on November tenth had been cancelled due to Ed's untimely death. Here is the article and a picture of Suzanne hugging your husband—there is no denying this. Look at this article."

"Oh lord the shame of this! The shame of it all!" cried Mrs. Eva.

"I wish shame was your only problem," said Mr. Kaufman. "Your husband was planning on your death and now someone has decided to rob you blind. Did you print the flyers for the slave auction?"

"No sir," she said.

"Do you know who did?"

"No sir."

"How are you having a slave auction and you don't know who printed the flyers announcing the auction? Someone paid for these flyers. Are you sure you did not receive a telegram about Ed's death?"

"No sir," she said crying softly, "this was the first time that I heard Ed was dead."

"Things are not right here Mrs. Eva. Tell me the major things that have happened since Ed left."

"The sheriff confiscated six hundred bales of my cotton, for Ed's debts. I have to see Judge Hargraves about the cotton after the auction.

"Banker Overton said Ed had taken a mortgage out on the plantation the day he left for New Orleans and it was due December fifteenth and if I did not have the mortgage money I would have to leave before Christmas. But Ed shouldn't have borrowed any money because he had the money we made from the tobacco harvest.

"I sold fifteen slaves to Master Brown so I could send my sister Amy to safety.

"Seven slaves ran for the freedom road; three were caught and I hung 'em.

"Banker Overton and his father are coming before the auction to make me an offer for the plantation land.

" I sold thirteen slaves to a man from New Orleans.

"Those are the main things that happened," she finished.

"Do you have the second mortgage? Did you sign for it?"

"No sir!"

"Did you get a telegram from your father that Ed was dead and to cancel the slave auction until spring?"

"No! No! NO!" she yelled.

"Eva, someone is trying to rob you blind. We will find out at lunch. Your father and brothers will be here about twelve thirty. Who brought you those slave flyers?"

"Flint Carter."

"Do you know where he got them?"

"He said they were posted on buildings in town and he took some down . . . and brought them to me . . . so I would know what Ed was doing."

"Well, my dear, we gonna find out the truth at lunch. Do you retain me as your lawyer?"

"Yes, I do."

"Then my fee will be five slaves of my choosing. Is it agreed?"

"Alright."

"Here, sign this contract. Now, go and put on your best dress and jewels. Then come downstairs and get ready to know the truth. Understand that when your father and you purchased this land it was bought in his name and your name only, not Ed's. Thus, Ed Smith could not have legally taken out a mortgage on the plantation without you and your papa's signature."

Jenny closed the stovepipe, gathered the dishes, and went into the kitchen. She was icing a coconut cake when Mr. Kaufman appeared.

"Jenny, I would like another slice of that chocolate cake."

"Yes sir," she said with a smile.

Mr. Kaufman sat at the kitchen table and ate every crumb of his cake, licked his fingers, and said,

"Jenny, where do you think I could find Overseer Graves this time of day?"

"He might be in the slave quarters, sir. I really do not know. Today, everyone is getting ready for the slave auction."

"Well, I will look for him there." As he was leaving, he said, "Take some food to the barn for Pete and the boys. They are helping me with my horse and I want to be sure they eat something."

"Yes sir, I will be more than happy to do it."

Mr. Kaufman left through the kitchen's back door and headed toward the barn to check on his horse. Old Sarah collected bits of foods, biscuits, and jam, and placed them in a pail, then said, "If Mrs. Eva was to ask for me, tell her I have gone to get eggs!"

"OK," said Jenny. "When are you coming back, Mama Sarah? I need to go to the barn for a minute."

"All right, child, I be back in a little while. I want to carry this little food to Grandmama Emma's folk. It sure a shame that Emma died today."

Jenny rushed around the house, making sure everything was perfect for the luncheon. She checked the downstairs parlor twice for any imperfection. She heard a knock on the kitchen door and there stood one of the biggest men she had ever seen. He was six feet nine inches tall and weighed more than 350 pounds. He had on a bearskin coat that made him look even bigger.

"Sorry if I frightened you, ma'am. Would you tell Eva that her mountain man cousin, Brock, is here?"

"Of course, sir," Jenny said.

"I ain't no sir," he said, with a smile that could melt snow off the mountain. "I is just Brock."

She ran upstairs and told Mrs. Eva that her cousin had arrived.

"Jenny, tell him I will be there in a few minutes. I have to finish getting ready. Be sure that everything is ready for the lunch."

"Yes, ma'am." Jenny ran down the stairs. "Mr. Brock, Mrs. Eva will be down in a few minutes. May I get you some breakfast?"

"I thought you would never ask," he said. "Do you think you could make me about half a dozen eggs, a large bowl of grits, a dozen biscuits, molasses, some coffee, and something sweet if you have it?"

"Why sure I can," said Jenny. "It will take me about half an hour to get it ready. Would you like to wait in the parlor?"

"No, I am not fittin' to sit in such a fancy place. I am going to walk over to the barn and look at your horses. I will be back by the time the food is ready."

Brock went to the barn and looked at the horses. He saw William and Daniel walking the mare and knew the horse was very sick.

"That horse of yours got colic—and she is with a foal as well."

"You are right," said Pete, as he turned to see who he was talking to him. "Brock, mountain man!" he yelled. "Brock, good morning. Thank you! Thank you! You saved my life back in the mountains."

"Slave Pete, I did not think you would make it. You had a terrible master. How did you get here on my cousin's plantation?"

"Is Mrs. Eva your cousin?"

"Why sure she is. She doesn't want folk to know but she and I are kin. What happened to the drunk man . . . Flint? I thought you belonged to him?"

"No sir! Flint Carter works for Mrs. Eva. He will be here sometime today for the slave auction."

"Oh! Are you going to be sold, slave Pete?"

"I am afraid so."

"That is too bad. What are you doing for this poor horse?"

"I am treating her for colic. If I can save the horse, a man named Kaufman promised to buy me and my family. And if I can save the foal, he promises to set me free."

"Let me help you!" Brock said.

Daniel yelled, "Old Grand Papa Pete, the horse is down! She is down!"

Both men raced to the horse and began to help her.

"Go and bring me some water, soap, and a funnel. We are going to give this horse an enema. We have to relieve the pressure in her middle," said Pete.

"This is going to get messy, but I will help you," said Brock.

"I am glad you are here. I do not have the strength needed to hold her down," said Pete.

They took the funnel, water, and soap and gave the horse an enema. They stepped back and waited for nature to take its course. A few minutes later a river of waste flooded the horse's stall. Both men were surprised to see that the horse had ingested large amounts of sand.

"Who would do such a thing to such a fine horse?" asked Brock. "It is clear someone was trying to kill this horse and foal."

"A man who would do such a thing to a horse should be hung," said Pete.

"Let us move the horse to another stall and get cleaned up. I almost forgot that Miss Jenny is cooking my breakfast. I'm going to eat it, but I will be back. Now that horse will be able to give birth to her foal—and I think it will happen soon." Brock left the barn and went to get his breakfast.

"Jenny, I thought you said Brock was here?"

"He is, Mrs. Eva. He went to the barn about an hour ago. Look, he is coming now."

"Hi, Cousin Eva. Miss Jenny has fixed me a beautiful breakfast and I would like to eat it here in the kitchen. Your papa sent word."

"Wait a minute, Brock. Jenny, take some food to Pete and the boys in the barn."

"Yes, ma'am, I will," she said slowly. She was shocked by Mrs. Eva's kindness. She fixed a bucket of food and left for the barn as quickly as possible.

"She is gone now. We can talk," said Mrs. Eva.

"Your papa sent a telegram to Beck Spur and told me to come and see about you. He said you were in some kind of trouble. So, I came as soon as I could. It was lucky that I was in Beck Spur getting provisions for the winter when the telegram arrived. I got the telegram and was able to save your man Pete's life."

"What did you say?" asked Eva.

"Yes, I saved his life. Your dad and your brothers will be here sometime today. He sent you a telegram. Did you get it? I am sorry Ed is dead."

"How did you know that Ed was dead?"

"It was in the telegram your father sent me a week ago. He said he was sending one to you."

"I never received a telegram."

"That is strange. Well, your father said to postpone the slave auction, and you are not to sign anything before he gets here. He also said he was sending Lawyer Kaufman to help you."

"Kaufman is here," she said. "Now tell me, how did you save Pete?"

"Well, the storekeeper's wife in Beck Spur asked me to look at a poor half-dead slave that had been chained to a post for almost a week. She said the man's jaw was broken and he could not eat, that he had been beaten and stomped when he objected to another slave being sold. A man named Flint Carter owned the slave, and said he had a right to sell the slave and the right to kill Pete if he had a mind to. He had spent the better part of a week drinking and gambling. Some say he lost over a thousand dollars. When I saw Pete, he had a sprained jaw, couple of cracked ribs, and his left eye was swollen shut. I did what I could.

"Each day that I was there, Carter would beat him for no reason. I could see Carter used a whip that had barbs in the leather. Those barbs tore poor Pete's flesh to bits. Frankly, I was surprise to see he was alive when I went to the barn. He says he is your slave. I do not understand how Flint Carter could sell one of your slaves and almost kill the other."

"I will explain later," she said. "Keep an eye out for my brothers."

"All right!"

"And Brock, go to the washhouse and tell Ella Mae that I said to get you a bath!"

When Mr. Kaufman arrived at the barn, he was so surprised that his horse looked better. He said again, "If you can save this horse, I will buy you and your family at the slave auction. And if you can save the foal, I will give you your freedom as well."

"Sir, you know my family includes five people: Old Sarah, Jenny, William, Daniel, and me."

"I know, I am a man of my word," said Mr. Kaufman. "Your family will do better off in Tennessee, with me!"

Pete asked God to help him. He prayed God would deliver them all. He had long ago stopped believing in the words of white men. It saddened his heart that a horse was worth more to Mr. Kaufman than five human beings. But his survival and the survival of those he loved depended on how he reacted to Mr. Kaufman.

"Thank you, sir! I will do what I can."

And with that Mr. Kaufman left the building.

Old Sarah heard what Pete said and she was in tears.

"Pete, do you think of me as family?"

"Of course, I do! You, the boys, and Jenny are the only family I have."

"Pete, if you save the foal or not, I got my freedom."

She pulled out some papers from her apron and said, "Mrs. Eva gave me my freedom papers two days ago. She promised that I would be free after the auction. Dr. Baker was there when she did it and he is a witness."

"May I see the papers?" asked William.

"Oh yes, son! Read it aloud for everyone. We family and we all know you can read."

Pete checked to see if they were alone and signaled William to read the papers.

Emancipation Papers

November 12, 1860

The slave known as Old Sarah on the Round Pond Plantation, owned by Master Ed and Mrs. Eva Smith, is a free person. Sarah's freedom begins ten days after the demise of Mrs. Eva Smith.

Signature _____Mrs. Eva Smith

Witness _____Dr. Eugene Baker

Mama Sarah was jumping up and down.

Daniel asked, "What does demise mean?"

"It means when someone dies."

"Mama Sarah, you have your freedom papers," said William, "but . . . but your freedom does not begin until ten days after Mrs. Eva is dead. I am afraid this is another one of Mrs. Eva's horrible jokes. To be free you have to outlive Mrs. Eva by ten days. You are twice her age and it is highly unlikely you will outlive her."

Upon hearing these words Mama Sarah fainted and fell to the floor as Jenny entered the barn.

"Oh Lord! What happened? What happened to Mama Sarah?"

"Aunty Jenny, she fainted when she . . . when she found out that her freedom papers are only good ten days after Mrs. Eva's death. She just fainted."

"Get me some water. Pete, take her to your room and lay her on the cot."

Slapping her face, placing cold compresses on her forehead, Jenny was finally able to revive Mama Sarah.

"Stop it! Stop it! That's enough, girl! Are you gonna slap me to death?"

"Oh, Mama Sarah, I thought you were dead."

" No not yet. Why all the long faces! Boys, go back and do your work."

"Mama, I would have never have read that part if I knew you would have fainted."

"William, I have a strong spirit, a surviving spirit. I am all right. I am relentless in my desire to survive. It is better to know the truth, no matter how painful, than to believe a sweet lie. You boys go back and do your work before someone finds out you are missing. Go now! Go on!"

"Pete, I have some news I need to tell you," Jenny said. "You and Mama Sarah."

"All right, Jenny. Spit it out."

"Mr. Ed is dead!"

"What!" said Pete.

"He died before he made it to New Orleans. Mr. Kaufman is a lawyer who came here to help Mrs. Eva. Telegrams have been sent to Mrs. Eva that she never got. Mr. Kaufman thinks somebody is trying to cheat Mrs. Eva. He has planned a big showdown. I think it will happen at lunch. I am afraid!"

"Do not be afraid! It has nothing to do with us. God will help us, I pray. Go back to the kitchen before you are missed," said Pete.

"Pete, would you have some white oleander?" asked Mama Sarah.

"Yes ma'am, I do."

"Kindly give me some. I have a need for it."

"All right," he said slowly. "Here it is."

She saw the sad look on his face and said, "Boy, I know more than you about white oleander and I ain't gonna kill myself."

Before Pete could utter another word, the barn doors flew open. Akbar was running for his life. Mr. Flint Carter was yelling and chasing him on the Arabian stallion. Carter was causing the horse to rear up and come down, trying to stomp the lad. When they came through the barn door the horse reared up. Pete thought he heard a swishing sound. Drunk Flint Carter hit his head on the door frame and fell on the floor.

"Up Kitty! Down Kitty!" a voice said, and the horse repeatedly stomped Flint Carter.

Overseer Graves came running into the barn.

"Pete! Pete, help!" he yelled. "Pete, take the stallion's reins. I think the man is dead. Did you see what happened?"

Akbar said, "Mr. Graves, he was chasing me and playing 'stomp the nigger.' Somehow, he lost his seat and fell and cracked his head open—and fell on his knife, I guess."

"Yes, that is about the jest of it," said Brock. "I saw him chasing the slave while I was on my way here to help Pete with Mr. Kaufman's mare."

"The man was drunk and out of control on most days. He has caused nothing but trouble since he has been here," said Graves. "Trying to kill a valuable slave on auction day!"

"Pete, take care of the horse. I will keep the knife," said Brock. "I could use a good one."

"Akbar, get some help and take Flint Carter's body to the pool house," Graves said. "I do not want anyone to see him until after the auction."

"Yes sir, Overseer Graves, we will do just that," said Pete.

"Well, I am headed to the washhouse. Eva wants me to take a bath," Brock said. "Which way is it?"

"It's over there. Do you see the little house where the tall woman is standing?" asked William.

"Yes, I do. It ain't every day I see a woman almost as big as me—and she's pretty too. Is she a white woman?"

"No sir, she's Ella Mae. But she don't tolerate men fooling around with her. The last man who tried, she flipped him flat on his back and said she will do the choosing when it is time for her to marry up with anyone."

Ben Brock laughed and walked toward the little house.

THE LUNCH

Jenny and Mama Sarah had prepared a lunch fit for a king. They had roast pork, turkey and stuffing, fried chicken, chicken with apricot sauce, oxtails and rice, potatoes, greens with poke salad, candied yams, peas, red beans and rice, corn bread, rolls, and numerous cakes and fried fruit pies. They made a wine punch for women, and plenty of the "product" was on hand for their husbands to drink. Jenny was worried about Mama Sarah, for the old woman had not said a word since they left the barn. She decided it was best to just leave her alone.

Knock! Knock! Knock!

People were arriving. Jenny ran to answer the door.

Mama Sarah put crushed oleander leaves in a pot, added hot water and chocolate, and slowly stirred the mixture. She added sugar, "the product," and milk. Then she took raw dried elderberries, mixed them with blackberry jam, placed this filling between white bread, and cut the bread into cute little sandwiches. She covered these special foods with a cloth and placed them on a shelf above the stove, waiting for an opportunity to give them to Mrs. Eva. The sandwiches would only give someone a harsh stomachache and diarrhea, but the chocolate and oleander would help Mrs. Eva meet Jesus.

The guests were arriving: Judge and Mrs. Hargraves; Pastor and Mrs. Roberts; Dr. Baker; old Ms. Cooper; Ms. Williams, the Anderson boys and their disgusting father; Banker Overton and his son; Mr. George, "the river rat"; Mr. and Mrs. Gamble who owned a store in Cross Junction; and Mr. and Mrs. Jones, the telegraph people. Jenny thought, What a strange mixture of people. The only people who had real money in this group were the Hargraves and the Overtons. But she invited them in the parlor to await Mrs. Eva.

Old Ms. Cooper said in a nasty tone, "Mrs. Jones, your shoes are caked with mud. Shows you are not used to coming to houses of quality. Jenny, take that woman to the kitchen and clean up her shoes before Eva sees this and throws her out."

Mrs. Jones was visibly upset. She followed Jenny into the kitchen. When Jenny knelt and tried to help her remove her shoes, she slapped the poor girl across her face with her riding crop.

"How dare that old woman embarrass me in front of everyone? She will see after today. Things around here are going to change. I'll show them," she muttered to herself.

Mama Sarah said, "Ma'am, let me take your coat." Then she removed the tray with the hot chocolate and sandwiches from the shelf and said, "May I serve you some hot chocolate and a little sandwich while you wait for your shoes? This is one of Mrs. Eva's special treats."

"Why yes," she said.

The greedy woman ate all the sandwiches and drank two cups of chocolate. She thanked Sarah and left the kitchen.

Meanwhile, Ben Brock knocked on the door of the washer's house. He said, "I am looking for Ella Mae. Mrs. Eva says you are to give me a wash."

"She did, did she? Well by the smell of you, you need one. But before we get started, understand a wash is all I am giving you."

"Oh no ma'am," said Brock softly, "I will not force myself on anyone. I am in need of a wash. And I need to change my clothes and be ready for the luncheon by eleven thirty."

"Well, come on in and let's get started. Go and shuck your clothes while I get the tub ready." She poured scalding hot water in a tub, then added more water, some soaking salts, and soap. She placed another log on the fire and said, "Come on out and get in—I am not looking. We do not have much time."

Ben Brock felt shy. He had been with a woman before, but he felt shy around Ella Mae— and slightly intimidated. She made his heart flutter. She smelled like sweet lavender. She moved with the quickness of a large mountain lion. He knew she could be fierce. She had a warrior's heart, and could probably beat most men, if given cause. She was all about business—and yet there was a softness in her.

As he looked around the small house, he could see she had filled it with love and natural things from the woods and forest: her dried flowers, the baskets she had made, the herb and rock garden in the window, the bits of rabbit skin she had sewn in her quilt. He was surprised how much he liked this woman.

She scrubbed him from top to bottom. Mounds of dirt filled the tub. He was embarrassed to be so dirty. She seemed to show no interest in him at all. This fact made him want her more. He appraised the woman, and he liked what he saw. She was big and well-shaped but not fat. Those hips! Lord, those hips! He loved her curves, the way she was plain talking, the little things she did, and how she hummed as she worked—and she had a wonderful smile when she thought no one was looking.

When he thought everything was done, he tried to get out of the tub. She laughed, and with one firm hold pushed his head under the water and scrubbed his hair.

"Now you did not think you were leaving here without your hair being washed," she said.

Normally, he would not have allowed anyone or anything to push him around. But he was enjoying this and was not in a hurry for her to finish. He smiled and said nothing.

Finally, she said. "I am going to step out now. Here is a towel. Dry off and get dressed.

When he heard the door close, he stood and dried himself, then put on his clean clothes. He had made up his mind that he was not leaving Round Pond Plantation until Ella Mae was by his side. Slave or no he was going to marry that woman. Maybe this was love at first scrub.

When he opened the door to leave the little house, she was sitting outside waiting for him to go.

"Miss Ella Mae, you need to tell everyone else you are taken. You is gonna be my wife!"

"Ben Brock, you been drinking too much moonshine. A white man can't marry a slave."

"Not in America, but in Canada, we can. And anyway, you look as white as any white woman I have ever seen. Got my mind set on it."

He picked her up as if she was a baby and this shocked her into silence. He then kissed her forehead and said, "You are gonna be Mrs. Ben Brock! My mind is set on it! And you might as well get ready."

"Put me down, Ben Brock," she said.

He gently placed her back in her seat, kissed her again on her forehead, and left for the Big House.

Mama Sarah, who watched the event from the kitchen porch, almost wet her pants.

"Lord look at you," she said, "causing folk to fall in love on a day like this. And the folk you chose—Ben Brock and Ella Mae."

She shook her head and went back into the kitchen!

Promptly at eleven thirty, everyone was invited into the dining room for lunch. At the head of the table sat Mrs. Eva, dressed as if she were a queen. She asked Judge Hargraves and his wife to sit on her left and Mr. and Mrs. Jones to sit on her right. The other guests took their seats and Mr. Kaufman sat at the end of the large table.

"Thanks everyone for coming. This will be a very trying day. I wanted us to meet and have lunch before the auction. I feel somewhat abandoned since I have not heard from my father nor my husband."

She motioned for the slaves to begin serving everyone. The slaves heaped mounds of food on each plate, and made sure everyone had plenty to drink. Ms. Cooper could not help noticing how much food Mrs. Jones was eating. Dr. Baker said quietly to Ms. Cooper that he would not be surprised if the woman ate herself to death, and they both laughed like little kids.

"Mr. Jones, has there been any telegram for me . . . from anyone?"

"No, Mrs. Eva, no telegram for you."

"Any telegrams about my husband?"

"I am sorry, ma'am, but no telegrams."

"Thank you," she said.

"Mr. George, I heard you and Ed were in New Orleans about the same time. Did you happen to see him? Or did you see Mr. Gamble or anyone from here? I am getting worried! Didn't you guys leave Cross Junction on the same boat, the Mississippi Queen?"

"Yes, Mrs. Eva, we left on the same boat, but I had a stop to make and got off the boat before it landed in New Orleans. I did not see Ed in New Orleans." Trying to distract her he said, "Mmm, mmm, this is mighty fine food. Best I had in a long time."

"Did you hear anything about him while you were there?" asked Mrs. Eva.

"No!" he said.

"Thank you, sir . . . I had to ask. Something horrible must have happened to him. As you all probably know, our cotton harvest was impounded by the sheriff for debts Ed accumulated while in New Orleans, and he even took out a mortgage on the plantation from Banker Overton while he was there. I was shocked and could not believe it. Thus, we are in a need of this slave auction today. Thank you again, friends, for coming," she said sweetly.

"Mr. Gamble, I understand you had your slave, Sam, put up flyers about the auction. I am obliged."

"It was the least I could do," said Gamble.

"I was wondering, where did you get those flyers? I did not have them printed. Maybe Ed sent them," she sighed. "Banker Overton, you have some paperwork for me. Let me have them so we can get that business over with."

"There, there!" said Lawyer Kaufman. "I will take that paperwork, Banker Overton. Let us retire to the library. Eva, play the piano for us."

She stood and said, "Come, join me in the library."

Eva sat at the piano and began playing. When everyone came into the library, tacked around the wall were newspapers from New Orleans. Each headline was more damning than the headline before.

- "Master Ed Smith from Cross Junction, North Carolina, killed on the Mississippi Queen," Nov 7, 1860
- "Socialite's wedding cancelled due to the death of her fiancé, Mr. Ed Smith," Nov 9, 1860
- "Mr. Ed Smith's body was identified by fellow townsmen, Gamble and George from Cross Junction, North Carolina," Nov 8, 1860

The voices in the room soon were louder than Eva's playing. Everyone was commenting on the news articles. Suddenly, the library doors slammed shut with a loud bang. Two shots were fired by Kaufman. Next to him stood Mrs. Eva's father, and at the back of the library were the sheriff, Overseer Graves, Eva's two brothers, and mountain man Brock with their guns at the ready.

Jenny, Old Sarah, and the other house servants heard the loud noise. They thought Mrs. Eva had kilt somebody this time for sure. The upstairs maid ran from the house!

"Victor!" Mama Sarah called.

"Mama Sarah, what is we going to do?" Victor asked.

Quietly she said, "You are gonna run, Victor—run for freedom. You will not get a better chance. If you stay here, you will be beaten, sold, or kilt. Better you run! Take the wood cart and the horse and go to the north field as if you are going to get firewood. Just like you and George do almost every day! And keep going north until you get to freedom! Follow the drinking gourd. Remember, moss grows on the northside of the tree.

"Come go with me."

"No son, I am too old. Take George with you." She took her medicine bag off her neck and gave it to him. She put some food and an old quilt in a cotton sack and said, "Go with God! Remember, drive the cart slowly until you get into the woods. As soon as you can, ditch the cart, and you and George ride the horse. He kissed Mama Sarah and walked out of the kitchen.

"George, get your coat. We got to git wood. Come on, let's go."

Suddenly, Jenny ran to the pantry to see if she could hear through the pantry walls what was going on in the library. She did not dare leave the kitchen.

Old Sarah sat by the pantry door and kept watch!

"Take a seat," she heard Kaufman command. "It is clear that some foul play has been going on here. Let us begin with you, Mr.

Jones. I have telegrams for your substation showing that you received telegrams for Eva that you never delivered. They involved the death of her husband and instruction from her father. Sir, these are federal crimes and you will be held for trial. Arrest him, Sheriff!

"Now Mr. George, would you like to explain how you can identify Ed Smith as being dead in New Orleans and not know he is dead when you arrive back in Cross Junction?"

Mr. George said not a word.

"Judge Hargraves, can you explain the validity of impounding six hundred bales of prime North Carolina cotton for gambling debts for dead Ed Smith. What evidence did you have? The only thing you shared with me was an IOU from Master Ed Smith dated six days after his death in New Orleans. That IOU is dated November fourteenth, and the IOUs belong to Mr. George and Sam Anderson. It is impossible for the dead to gamble with the living and sign an IOU. Gentleman, this is called fraud and you will be held by the sheriff until your trial. Judge Hargraves, I suggest that you sign a release of the cotton today to Mrs. Eva before her father and brothers take matters into their own hands."

Judge Hargraves looked across the room at Mrs. Eva's brothers, swallowed hard, and quickly looked at the floor.

"Last but not least: Banker Overton, I hold in my hand the mortgage you said Ed Smith requested by telegram three days after his death. This mortgage is dated November tenth. And today, you offered to buy this plantation for pennies. Clearly, Ed Smith did not come back from the dead and telegram you to send him money. Bank fraud is a federal crime. You and your son are going to jail."

The younger Overton said, "Papa made me do it! I can't go to jail!"

"Son, son, be a man and take your punishment," said Overton Senior.

"No, I won't!" he said.

"Now wait a minute—one of the main people in trying to get Mrs. Eva's money was Flint Carter. He even sold one of her slaves without her knowledge and he killed that free black man who owned that fine Arabian horse. (John Francis Bernard Kaufman heart sank…He knew his beloved son Clifford was dead…but he did not react nor show any emotions.) Where is Flint Carter?" asked Sam Anderson.

"I am sorry to say," answered Lawyer Kaufman, "but Mr. Carter had a riding accident and he is dead. (May he rest in hell, thought Kaufman). Nevertheless, Mrs. Eva owes you nothing. This has been a big conspiracy to defraud this poor southern belle of her home and property. The shame of it all. You have no claim on this property! Let me be perfectly clear that you have no claim to the plantation, the cotton, nor the slaves! The circuit judge will be here in a week to ten days. You are all going to be held for trial. One of you will be tried for the murder of Ed Smith."

Another Anderson cried out, "Judge Hargraves and the Overtons set this up! And George killed Ed!"

"Save it for court," said Kaufman. "Save it for the court, son."

The sheriff handcuffed the men and took them to jail.

"Women, you can see the judge about bail tomorrow morning," he said as he took them away.

"Well, that settles it," said Eva. "Now ladies, I suggest you follow your husbands and get the hell off my plantation!"

Her father laughed and said, "That's my girl!" Heaved his handgun in direction of the door and had another drink.

CHAPTER SEVENTEEN

New Beginnings

"Now Eva, it is past time I get back to my beloved Tennessee."

"Thank you, Lawyer Kaufman," said her dad. "We will double whatever Eva promised."

"The promise was five slaves of my choosing."

"Very well," he said.

"And I will need two wagons and supplies. I am willing to buy those."

"No need," said her father, "that is on the house. Right Eva?"

"Yes, Papa," she said.

"Thanks!" said Kaufman. "Would it be ok if Old Sarah went with me as well? Eva has given the old woman her freedom papers, and she has no place to go. Is it all agreeable?"

"It certainly is!" said her father.

"Then we will be on our way before nightfall. All I need is a bill of sale for the slaves and horses and a gift deed for Old Sarah."

"Eva, make out the bill of sale and gift deed for Mr. Kaufman. This is a great deal! You have a famous name, property, wealth, and you are rid of a husband you did not want," her father said as he smiled and began to smoke his cigar. "Oh, what a great day! What a great day for the Gaines clan!"

Bill of Sale for Slaves

December 15, 1860

Slaves	*Age*	*Sex*	*Value/price*
Pete	45 years	male	2500.00
Jenny	30 years	female	1200.00
William	11 years	male	1000.00
Daniel	16 years	male	1600.00
Manny	35 years	male	1600.00
China	26 years	female	1200.00
Akbar	20 years	male	1000.00
Otis	29 years	male	1400.00
Ella Mae	18 years	female	1400.00
Becca	11 years	female	600.00

Sold to John Francis Bernard Kaufman of Brownville, Tennessee December 15, 1860.

Mrs. Eva Gaines Smith

Round Pond Plantation

Cross Junction, North Carolina

Witness Sheriff Baldwin Owens

Witness Mr. James Jethro Gaines

Deed of Gift

The slave known as Old Mary, approximately seventy-two years old, is deeded to John Bernard Kaufman by Mrs. Eva Gaines Smith.

December 15, 1860

Signed: Mrs. Eva Gaines Smith
Witness: Mr. James Jethro Gaines

Bill of Sale

Livestock

Eight horses	Value	$3000.00

Equipment

Two covered wagons	$900.00
Food and supplies	$500.00

Eva Smith

Round Pond Plantation

Cross Junction, North Carolina

The sheriff loaded up the men in the jail wagon and covered the wagon with a tarp and told their wives they would need to see the circuit judge about bail.

Jenny eased out of the pantry and looked to see if anyone was around. Then she told Old Sarah, "We have been bought by Mr. Kaufman. Put on every thang you own except your coat. Put your coat, sewing kit, healing herbs, and some bandages in your bedroll and tie it tightly. If Mrs. Eva allows us to go, she will say we can only take the clothes on our back and our bedroll."

Old Sarah nodded and began to gather her things.

"Be careful," warned Jenny, "make sure no one sees you."

CHAPTER EIGHTEEN

High Hopes

Lawyer John Francis Bernard Kaufman was quite proud of his work. He gathered his documents and went upstairs to pack his things to leave. He was slightly annoyed that Eva never said thank you for all his work. But it was enough that his friend, her father, was grateful.

He was even more surprised that Mrs. Eva and her family had decided to have the slave auction after all. Eva and her brothers were talking to the auctioneer and people who had come to the auction. The slaves were putting out the free food. He did not see his men out front or at the food table. He was again surprised and wondered where they were.

When he came downstairs, his right-hand man Roger was waiting for him.

"Get the others," he said, "and let's go."

"Mrs. Eva sent the men to town with the sheriff. I thought you knew. She said we would be leaving tomorrow and the men would be spending the night in town. I thought you OKed it, sir."

Evil Eva never stops, Kaufman thought.

"She sent up two apricot brandies, one for you and one for her dad. Old Sarah was supposed to bring them. I guess the old slave has not made it up the stairs."

"That's fine," he said. "Go tell Mrs. Eva that I am taking a nap and that I asked you to pack the supplies so we can leave early in the morning. Then take my horse and the supplies to the barn. Be quick about it. I will meet you in the barn in thirty minutes."

Kaufman took his bag and went into the kitchen.

"Jenny and Sarah, I have bought you from Mrs. Eva. You have five minutes to get your things and leave with me."

"Old Sarah, Roger said you were bringing me some apricot brandy. I could use a drink about now."

"Lawyer Kaufman," she said, "Apricot brandy ain't always good for you. Sometimes people get white oleander and apricot confused. It is easy to do. They smell almost the same. But I know the difference. Somehow, Mrs. Eva's dog got hold of the drinks she sent you and her father and that poor dog has gone to meet Jesus! If you need a drink sir, I suggest you drink some of the 'product.'"

When he heard what Sarah said, Kaufman's eyes got as big as a saucer. He looked at the dog and knew the poor thing was dead. He knew Eva had planned to kill him and her father. He said, "Thank you, Sarah. Ladies no time to pack. Come as you are."

Jenny and Old Sarah picked up their bedrolls and followed Kaufman to the barn.

At the barn, Kaufman said, "Pete, I bought your family—Jenny, William, Daniel, and you. Mama Sarah is coming as a gift. Also, I purchased part of Manny's family: Manny, his wife China, their daughter Becca, and their son Akbar and his brother Otis. Additionally, I bought Ella Mae.

"Now listen closely: we must leave here within the hour or less. I want to leave just as soon as the auction starts at two. That gives us about thirty minutes to get packed and go. I will not wait for anyone. Do you understand!"

Pete selected eight strong ponies and two covered wagons that could travel to Tennessee. He hitch a four-horse team to each wagon. He got extra tarp to cover the back and front wagon openings.

"Jenny, tell Ella Mae I said come to the barn and bring as many blankets and quilts as she can. Have her place these items in one of her big laundry baskets. Make sure her coat is in the basket as well. If anyone asks what you are doing, just say a horse needs tending and you have been sent to help. Come back to the barn. Then leave through Pete's room and go to the weaver's cabin and get China and her daughter," Kaufman said.

"Daniel, go and find Manny, Otis, and Akbar and tell them to come to the barn," He continued. "Do this quietly and quickly. I do not want people to notice we are leaving. Do not run or draw attention to yourselves."

Kaufman took a good look at William and said, "William, I do not want you to leave the barn. If Mrs. Eva's father sees you, he will kill you because you look just like Ed Smith. Go into Pete's room and pack all the herbs and plants that are in the room, any food supplies, rope, tools, and blankets. Then bring those things here so we can put them in the wagon. Then get in the wagon and hide under some blankets."

Daniel knew exactly where Otis, Manny, and Akbar were. He went to the tobacco shed to collect them. When he saw the men, he said, "Manny and Otis, go to the barn! Hurry! See Pete when you get there. He needs your help! Akbar, come with me."

Next Daniel and Akbar went to the north field and collected Mr. Kaufman's string of horses and the Arabian stallion he had hidden in the forest. They brought the horses to the barn's back entrance, got rope, and prepared the horses for travel. Daniel went into Pete's room to get his things and told Akbar to go in the barn and see Pete.

Jenny went and got Ella Mae. Ella Mae put food, knives, an axe, and ten to twelve quilts in one of her large laundry baskets.

"Take those things to the barn," said Jenny. "Then come to the weaver's cabin. Hurry!"

Ella Mae dropped the basket off at the barn and went the back way to the weaver's cabin. She and Jenny arrived at the same time. When they entered the weaver's cabin, they saw China was in labor. Jenny froze.

But Ella Mae said, "Girl, tell that baby to hold on. We have been bought by Mr. Kaufman and we are on our way to Tennessee. I do not know what Tennessee is like but anything is better than this hellhole. Kaufman will not wait. We must get to the barn. You must bear the pain and come or stay and be sold without your family. He bought Manny, your son, and your daughter."

"What about Emanual?"

"He didn't say. But we ain't leaving this baby. Becca, put on everything you can wear. I am going to gather all the quilts and blankets I can find," said Ella. "Jenny, you and China go to the barn. The kids and I will follow."

"Emmanual, do you like games?"

"Yes," said the three-year-old.

"Well, this is a quiet game. I am going to put you in a sack and place that sack over my arm and around my neck. Then I am going to put a hole in a quilt and place the quilt over you and I. Put your arms around me and hold tight. No matter what happens, you must not speak, sneeze, cough, or move. If anyone finds out that I am taking you, it will cause a lot of trouble. The master will whip me—or worse," she said.

"I will not make a sound," said the little boy. "I don't want you to get in trouble and I don't want to be left alone."

"Becca you hold one basket handle and I will hold the other."

Slowly, Ella Mae, Emanual, and Becca headed toward the barn. Becca and Ella Mae were talking and laughing as they went along and Emanuel said not a word.

Ben Brock had been scouring the plantation looking for his beloved Ella Mae. He was beside himself when he heard she had been sold to Kaufman. The moment he saw her he knew something was wrong. For one thing, she wasn't that big in her middle. What was that woman up too, he thought? He started to come to her but she looked at him and he knew to stop. He watched as she entered the door to Pete's room in the barn. And he waited.

Pete had the teams and the wagons ready. He and Roger had loaded the food supplies and some building tools Pete kept in the barn, along with an axe and shovel. He made sure his flint rocks were in the bag he wore at his side and he placed his killing club under the wagon seat. Then he tied a water barrel to each wagon.

Kaufman said, "I am not going to force you to go with me by chaining you up. If you want to go, get in the wagon and keep quiet. If you want to stay here and be with Mrs. Eva, God bless you. We must leave now."

Pete took charge and said, "I will drive the first wagon. Manny will drive the second wagon. Daniel will ride the Arabian stallion. Akbar and Otis will lead Mr. Kaufman's string of horses. China, Jenny, Old Sarah and I will ride in the first wagon. William, Becca, and Ella Mae will ride in the second wagon. This will balance the load. Tie the mare to the second wagon. Put what we have gathered in the wagons and let's go."

Within five minutes they were all set to go. Pete double checked the wagons and tied the tarps over the back and front of each wagon so no one could see in.

They could hear that the slave auction had started. It had a festive atmosphere. The buyers were ready to begin. Rich slave owners came to buy the best craftsmen, or strongest men, or the prettiest slaves. However, some poor whites who could not afford a slave came to the slave auction as if they were going to a fair. They watched, ate the free food, drank moonshine, gambled, made fun of the slaves, and waited to participate in the shooting games. For some, it was the only way they could feel important. Even if they did not have any money and were half starving, a slave auction reaffirmed that they were better than a "nigger" in their minds. Others used slave auctions to make money and to see friends and family.

It was a strange mixture of cries, laughter, joy, and untold sorrow. The auctioneer was performing his function, singing his strange song. They heard him speak, halfway singing: "I have a prime female slave here named Mary Ann. Look at her legs! Pull up your skirt, girl. Higher! Look at those long, strong, fine legs. Show the men your chest. Take off that blouse. Turn around! Turn around, I said! Put your hands down so they can get a good look at you!" She hesitated and the overseer struck her with his whip and she dropped her hands.

"There, there, stop your crying. You know you ain't got no feelings! Who will bid five hundred dollars for this prime young girl slave? She is fifteen and will be a good breeder.

"Five hundred over here—who will give five fifty for this slave? Five fifty here! Six hundred? Six hundred hundred to my right. Seven hundred dollars! Seven hundred to the lady in the back. This a fine specimen of womanhood. Eight hundred dollars, anyone? Eight hundred going once—eight hundred going twice—sold! Sold to young Mr. James Curtis from Manor House Plantation here on the left. Pay the cashier, sir, and collect your slave."

No words could or can express the acute, soul-chilling sorrow felt by the slave being sold. Yet part of her anguish was felt by the whole human race. She had been ripped from all she knew, treated less than an animal, and stripped naked before her father, brothers, uncles, and male cousins. And none of them could protect her or come to her defense.

White men and women feasted on her nakedness as if she was food to be devoured. Their inhumanity and indifference toward her threw her deeper in the hellhole called slavery via this slave auction. And yet they could not see that this slave auction would cause damage to their souls for generations to come. For it is written, you will reap what you sow!

Would she drown or swim! Would her spirit survive? Could she control the only thing that was truly hers, her mind? Would she have a surviving spirit! Would she be relentless? Or would she allow the pain she felt in her body and mind make her become one of the living dead, just going through the motions. Only she knew the answer.

For now, she was relieved to be able to pull down her skirt, cover her chest with her hands, and step down from the auction block with the serenity of a queen. As she made the first step she looked up and saw her mother and remembered her last words, "Survive, survive—one day black children will be rulers in this world. You must be relentless! It is written in the stars. No matter how hard it gets. You must survive! As long as black children survive, we will never die."

She lifted her head, nodded toward her mother, and said to herself, "Nothing but God will keep me from it. I, Mary Ann will survive! I shall be relentless in my desire for freedom."

* * * *

Quietly the caravan left the barn and the sounds of the auction and moved down the back road of the plantation. Pete led the way driving the first wagon. He took a slow and steady pace. Manny drove the second wagon. Kaufman's man Roger, William, and Akbar drove the horses, staying just to the left of the wagons. Five minutes behind everyone rode Mr. Kaufman. And away they went.

Ben Brock went to the barn to search for his beloved Ella Mae. When he did not find her, he knew she was in the caravan. He wondered why Kaufman was secretly leaving the plantation. He saddled his horse, gathered his gear, closed the barn doors, and followed the caravan. He was hell-bent and determined to marry Ella Mae. But now the wisest thing to do was to follow the caravan and do all he could to keep her safe.

Illustrations

Nozomi Ann Johnson

www.ingramcontent.com/pod-product-compliance
Lightning Source LLC
LaVergne TN
LVHW041845070526
838199LV00045BA/1452